Emma
on
thin
icing

SIMON SPOTLIGHT

An imprint of Simon & Schuster Children's Publishing Division
1230 Avenue of the Americas, New York, New York 10020
Copyright © 2011 by Simon & Schuster, Inc. All rights reserved,
including the right of reproduction in whole or in part in any form.
SIMON SPOTLIGHT and colophon are registered trademarks
of Simon & Schuster, Inc. Text by Elizabeth Doyle Carey.
Designed by Laura Roode.
For information about special discounts for bulk purchases,
please contact Simon & Schuster Special Sales
at 1-866-506-1949 or business@simonandschuster.com.
Manufactured in the United States of America 0213 OFF
8 10 9 7
ISBN 978-1-4424-2279-7
ISBN 978-1-4424-2280-3 (eBook)
Library of Congress Control Number 2011935643

CUPCAKE DIARIES

Emma
on
thin
icing

by coco simon

Simon Spotlight
New York   London   Toronto   Sydney

CHAPTER 1

Everything Is Better with Bacon

My name is Emma Taylor, and my life can be pretty hectic sometimes. I have three brothers, four goldfish, a guinea pig, and two jobs. Yup, two businesses. The first is a dog-walking job I have after school. My other job isn't really a job. It's a club with my best friends—Alexis, Katie, and Mia. Together we're the Cupcake Club. We bake and sell cupcakes for different people and events. It's totally fun, but we don't earn that much money . . . yet.

Between my brothers, chores, and the club, things can get pretty crazy. Most of the time, though, being in the middle of all this craziness can mean getting some pretty great inspirations. Like the one I had about bacon. Bacon cupcakes. Trust me, they're great. They're salty with the bacon and sweet with the sugar and the combination is really the best. It just *sounds* gross. I had been waiting to bring it up until just the right time, so finally, at our club meeting, I decided to see how it would fly. We were talking about new ideas because we're always trying out new things, depending on the event. I was a little nervous, but I decided to float the idea.

"Okay, ready? How about . . . bacon cupcakes?" I asked.

I spread my arms wide in an arc—like "ta-da"—as I announced my idea. I wasn't sure how the others would react to it, but I thought it was pretty neat. And original. That was for sure. I just hoped they didn't think I was nuts.

"Ewwww!" cried Katie, with a full-body shudder.

"Are you kidding me?" Alexis looked so horrified, you would have thought I had suggested roadkill cupcakes.

I just shrugged. I knew better. "My brothers loved them. I made them last week. Actually, they're delicious. Kind of salty and sweet. Think about it."

Unlike the other members of the Cupcake Club, Mia was quiet, and she looked like she was actually considering the idea. Finally she said "I love bacon *and* cupcakes, but I've never thought about them together. Bacon is kinda in right now. There's bacon gum, bacon mayonnaise, bacon ice cream, bacon-shaped Band-Aids. It would be pretty cool to have bacon cupcakes."

Mia was pretty hip. She had long, straight, dark hair and really cool outfits, and was from Manhattan. I have no idea how she knew what was "in" or what wasn't, but we all pretty much listened when she said something was in. So Katie and Alexis stopped their dramatic groaning and belly-clutching and listened.

Seeing that I was making headway with my idea, I forged on. "I was thinking, maybe for the groom's cake. You know how they do that? Have a special cake on the side for the men? It's kind of a Southern thing. The bride has her own cake and the groom has his."

"Like an extra order?" asked Katie.

I nodded and looked a little guiltily at Mia. "Not that I want to make money off your mom or anything."

"Emma, you may have just doubled our revenue!" said Alexis, ever the businesswoman. She raised her glass of Gatorade in a toast. I smiled and raised my glass back at her. Alexis actually did look like a businesswoman right now with her red hair up in a bun and a sensible button-down shirt, holding a calculator and a pad of paper.

The Cupcake Club was meeting in Mia's cozy room to brainstorm about upcoming jobs. One of our next big events was Mia's mom's wedding to Eddie, her supernice fiancé. We were all excited for Mia because Eddie was great and her mom was really happy. But we were also excited for ourselves because Mia's mom had placed an order with the club for cupcakes for the wedding! She had given us the green light to do whatever we thought was appropriate. And I thought bacon cupcakes were appropriate. Best of all, she would pay us for the order.

Alexis was taking notes. "Okay, let me just read this back to you. One idea is a circular cupcake wedding cake built with three sizes of cupcakes to make up the tiers—our medium, large, and jumbo sizes building out the cake, with a few minis on top. The cake would be white, the frosting white buttercream. Decorations would be white flowers molded from edible fondant. Cupcake papers would be shiny and white." She looked up at the other Cupcake Club members for confirmation. We all nodded, and she looked back at her notes.

"Another idea is to do all minis laid out in a large sheet, mostly white cake and white frosting but with select cupcakes frosted in pink raspberry frosting and placed to form the shape of a heart in the middle of the layout." Again, we nodded. The mini cupcakes were very popular; they were not much bigger than a quarter and they could be consumed easily in vast quantities.

Alexis continued. "We will also submit a bid for a groom's cake made of . . . um, bacon cupcakes. These are . . . what kind of cake?"

"Caramel cake," I said. My mouth was watering just thinking of it. "And the frosting is just a standard buttercream with flecks of real bacon in it. It comes out sort of beige."

Alexis shuddered. "Okay. Beige cupcakes. I will do an analysis on head count and budget and come up with a cupcake count so we can submit our bids to your mom by the end of the week. I'll e-mail it to everyone for approval first. Especially the bacon cupcake part. Then we can meet and go over it again."

We nodded in agreement.

"Next on the agenda is—"

"Wait!" interrupted Mia, her eyes shining with excitement. "I have great news." She clasped her hands together.

I restrained myself from looking at my watch.

I didn't want to be rude, but I prided myself on being extremely punctual and organized and I had to be at the Andersons' to walk Jenner, their retired greyhound rescue dog, at four o'clock. It had to be almost three forty-five now. I really hated to be late. I also didn't want to lose the dog-walking job. In fact, I couldn't afford to.

Meanwhile Mia had paused for effect. Then taking a deep, dramatic breath she announced, "My mom wants us all . . . the four of us . . . to be junior bridesmaids at the wedding!" Mia jumped up on the couch and started to hop up and down with excitement, swinging her arms.

"Oh my gosh!" cried Katie, jumping up after her. "I've never even been to a wedding, never mind *in* one!" She jumped up and down too.

"Me neither!" I cried. I jumped up on the couch, since it appeared that was how we were celebrating. I caught a glimpse of Katie's watch in midair as her arm sailed past. Three forty-nine. *Could I leave now? No, that would be rude.* I had to stick it out for five more minutes to enjoy the news with the other girls. And it *was* good news.

"That is excellent," said Alexis definitively. She was not the couch-jumping type, but we loved her anyway.

6

"Your mom is so cool," I said. Then I felt bad. My mom was cool too, but she'd been distracted and out of touch the past couple of weeks because she'd gotten furloughed, or suspended, from her job at the town library due to government cutbacks. Basically they'd told her to go home until they could come up with some money to pay her. Last week she'd finally had to take a part-time job at the bookstore at the mall just to have some extra income. But the hours were terrible and our family's routines and schedules had been turned upside down. This was bad because I love a schedule, and I get really jumpy and grumpy when my schedules get messed up. My dad had given me and my three brothers a pep talk about how we had to stick together and pitch in and not worry Mom or put any pressure on her. It was hard. But I was nothing if not dependable. "I know I don't have to worry about you, Emma," Mom would always say. And I made sure she really didn't have to worry about me now. But I missed seeing Mom and having her there when I got home after school. She was always running around these days. To be honest I wasn't sure my mom even remembered what the Cupcake Club was, let alone how important it had become to us.

It had all started on the first day of middle school, when we sat together at lunch, and we stared at Katie's delicious homemade cupcake. The next day she brought in cupcakes to share and they were good. Really good. It was Alexis's idea to bring cupcakes every Friday, and we all took turns. We all banded together then. We stuck together when Sydney Whitman formed the Popular Girls Club and none of us were in it. We started to bake together and then formed a business. The Cupcake Club took off, and we began making cupcakes for events all over town. It was sometimes a lot of work, but it was also a lot of fun.

"So what are we going to wear?" asked Katie.

Mia's mom worked in fashion, so the question of the bridesmaid dress was sure to get a great deal of discussion. "Well, we just started talking about it, and we didn't get too far before she had to leave for work," said Mia. "She's going to pick up some bridal magazines for ideas, and we can all look at them. Then we might go to the bridal salon where she got her dress and try stuff on."

"Fun!" said Alexis. "Have you ever been?"

"Yes, I was there when my mom went to try on her wedding dress for the first time . . . ," began Mia, warming to the topic.

8

I wanted to stay and listen, but I started getting antsy. I had not budgeted time for this and now I was stuck here for another ten minutes at least, discussing the various types of wedding dresses and junior bridesmaid dresses. And worse, I knew that if we had to buy dresses for the wedding, it would be a big expense. Since my mom had lost her job, there hadn't been any money for extras. There was hardly enough money for clothes or sporting goods. (In a house with three brothers, sporting goods were as much of a basic necessity as food. Things were always getting lost or being outgrown.) We had to earn extra spending money for movies and pizza and things like that, which is why I started walking Jenner. I tried to save most of my dog-walking money, though. I had been saving up for so long for a pink KitchenAid mixer I'd seen in the Williams-Sonoma catalog. We were the only ones who didn't have a fancy mixer, and baking at our house was such a pain when someone had to use the old hand-held one we had. Oh no. Would I have to spend all the money on a bridesmaid's dress?

"What do you think?" asked Mia, turning to me.

"Huh?" I said. I had been thinking about my savings account.

"Earth to Emma! You've been such a space cadet

lately!" chided Katie with a smile. "Are you bored of us?"

I could feel my face get red. "I guess I should be eating more cupcakes to keep my energy up," I joked. It was just that I had so much to keep track of: school, flute practice (I'm in the school orchestra), Cupcake Club, my new job walking the neighbors' dog, and babysitting my younger brother. It was getting to be a lot. I hadn't told anyone about my mom's job or how I had to babysit Jake more or how many conversations we had about saving money at my house.

"Oh no! Am I rambling on too much?" asked Mia, embarrassed. "You know I could talk about fashion all day!"

I instantly felt rotten about putting any kind of damper on what should have been a great moment for Mia. I didn't want her to think I wasn't excited.

"No, you're not rambling at all! And I am so psyched about your mom's wedding. I think it's so cool that we get to do the cupcakes, and I am so excited about us being junior bridesmaids. It's so amazing." I really did mean it. It was great news.

Mia smiled. "Thanks! I can't wait!"

"It's just . . ." I wanted to tell my best friends about our money troubles, but I just couldn't. It would be embarrassing, not to mention kind of disloyal to my family. And anyway, I didn't want to lay it all out and then have to run out the door and potentially leave them all talking about me and feeling sorry for us Taylors. "It's just that I have to go home and watch Jake. And I'm worried I'm going to be late for his bus! But I don't want to run out on all this great news! I want to talk about all the dresses, but then I'll be late!"

Well, it wasn't a total lie. I did have to watch Jake, but not until tomorrow, when my brother Matt had basketball practice. It was his turn to watch Jake after school today. Running out on them for Jake sounded more legitimate than running out on them for a dog, that's all.

"Oh no! Go! We're totally done," said Mia sweetly.

"What about the Garner job? The four-year-old's birthday party? We need to submit a bid for that . . . ," said Alexis.

I froze. I was halfway to standing up, and I plunked back down on the couch. The club rule was that we all had do to the planning together so no one got stuck with it (even though I secretly thought Alexis would totally be okay doing all of it).

But Mia waved. "Go, go. You can't be late! We'll

e-mail you what we come up with, okay?"

I was torn. I hated feeling like this. "Really?" I knew I was biting my lip.

"Go! It's fine!" said Katie nicely. "Really!"

I looked at Alexis, and she nodded.

"Okay," I said. "Sorry." I gave Mia a big hug. "Just let me know the details . . ." Then I grabbed my backpack and hustled out.

I am going to be so late, I thought as I dashed out of Mia's house, which I loved. Everything here was so stylish and neat and clean in contrast to my house, where everything was sturdy enough for three boys and slightly trashed and of questionable cleanliness. Just yesterday I had to kick three pairs of Matt's disgustingly stinky socks off the sofa before I sat down.

I clipped my bike helmet on and hopped on my bike. Well it was mine now. It was a hand-me-down from Sam, my eldest brother, by way of Matt, the next one down. It was a boys' bike, with a bar, and it was gray and a little too big for me. But it was in decent shape and totally reliable. I pumped hard for the seven blocks home, standing up on the pedals almost the whole way, and taking the most efficient route.

I passed Jake's bus, which was stopped on the

block before our house. Flying by at top speed, I just waved at all of the windows. One of them had to be Jake's. I turned up the driveway, ditched my bike in the rack so I didn't get yelled at for leaving it out, ran into the mudroom and dumped my backpack and flute case into my locker (yes, we actually have lockers at home; it is the only way to contain the madness, my mom says), and was about to dash back out to get Jenner for his walk.

"Where have you been?" Matt screeched. He went flying past me out the door, dressed in his basketball uniform with his jacket over it, the jacket flapping open in his haste. His light, curly hair was smushed under a baseball hat and his blue eyes flashed with impatience.

"What?" I asked, not comprehending. I followed him out to the driveway.

"They changed my practice time!" yelled Matt, hopping on a bike. *My bike!*

"Wait, that's my bike!" I yelled. "And what about Jake?"

"He's all yours! Mom said! And it used to be my bike so I still can claim it!" And Matt went sailing off.

The bus pulled up, and Jake shuffled out. His shaggy blond hair was all messed up and his blue

13

eyes looked tired. He had on jeans and his favorite T-shirt; it was blue and said NYPD.

"Bye, buddy!" called Sal, the driver. Sal waved at me. I sighed and waved back. This was not what I bargained for.

"Hi, Emmy," said Jake as he trudged up the driveway. His backpack was bigger than his whole back. I couldn't imagine what he carried in it besides his lunch.

"Hi, pal." I sighed again and took a deep breath. I didn't want to snap at him. It wasn't Jake's fault Matt had ditched him. It wasn't his fault that Mom had a new part-time job so she couldn't be home to meet him after school.

I thought about how I was going to negotiate this. Jake requires careful planning. "I'll grab you a quick snack while you use the bathroom and then we'll go walk Jenner real quick, okay?" I said, trying to keep my voice light. Jake could be a bit of a tyrant, and if he wasn't in the mood to do something, there was no way he'd do it. It was a little like taking care of a puppy.

"But I'm tired!" whined Jake, his shoulders drooping. "I just wanna stay home and watch TV!"

I could see the Jenner walking job slipping away, and I couldn't let that happen. I had to think fast.

"You can bring your scooter and . . . we'll go to Camden's, and I'll buy you a piece of candy!" It would cost me, but it would be worth it.

Jake paused as if weighing his options: tantrum or candy. I held my breath. Finally he spoke. "Two pieces."

Phew. "Two pieces it is, mister, but hustle now. Poor Jenner is crossing his little doggy legs, he needs to pee so badly!"

This sent Jake into peals of laughter, and I knew I had him. And it was only 4:10.

One problem at a time conquered with a little planning. *That's how we roll, baby,* I said to myself as I hustled us out the door. *That's how we roll.*

CHAPTER 2

Dogs and Brothers Don't Mix

Jenner leaped excitedly behind the Andersons' door as I got the key from its hiding place and put it in the lock at 4:20. Jake watched the dog closely through the window with wide eyes. Jenner could be as much of a handful as Jake sometimes.

"You stay here, Jakey, while I go in and get his leash on, okay?" I said. Once he was on his leash Jenner would be fine.

Jake nodded. He didn't hate dogs, but he wasn't crazy about them either. Especially big, excited ones.

Sliding my knee through the opening in the door, I forced Jenner gently backward, then pulled the door shut. He was a good dog, but a little energetic at first.

"Hey, boy! Hi, buddy!" Jenner jumped up and tried to put his two front paws on my shoulders. I grabbed him firmly by the collar and spoke to him in a soothing voice and patted his head. It had taken a few tries, but I learned that you just had to be very calm with him. Kind of like when you were talking to Jake on the verge of a meltdown. Sure enough, Jenner stopped jumping, and I grabbed the leash from the hook and clipped it to his collar. Then I picked up the pooper-scooper Baggies holder and put it in my pocket. All set.

I looked around before I left. The Andersons' mudroom was so neat, with everyone's shoes in individual cubbyholes and the Anderson girls' jackets and sporting equipment neatly aligned. I loved organization. I inhaled deeply. Something smelled really good. *Mmm,* I thought. Beef bourguignonne—a savory stew. Mom used to make it a lot. Mrs. Anderson worked full time at an insurance agency so, because of her schedule, she was a big Crock-Pot aficionado. A Crock-Pot cooked all day, and every time you came into the house you smelled dinner. Lately we ate mostly microwave stuff. It didn't smell nearly as good.

Jenner gave a short bark, and I realized I had been standing there for a minute. "That's a good boy, now. Time for your walky," I said. Poor guy. He probably really had to go.

I opened the door, and Jenner charged out, yanking on the leash. "Easy, boy," I said. Then I turned to find Jake, but he wasn't standing where I had left him.

"Jake?" I called. Where could he have disappeared to so quickly?

Jenner pulled on the leash toward the sidewalk where we usually go, but I thought Jake must be in the Andersons' backyard. They had a swing set and that would have captured his attention. I pulled Jenner along and peered over the low, white picket fence into the backyard. No Jake. Uh-oh. He could only have headed down the driveway to the sidewalk. Now I felt a little nervous.

"C'mon, Jenner," I said, and we trotted quickly down the driveway to the street. I looked left. No Jake. Then I looked right and there, way off in the distance about two blocks ahead, was Jake, motoring along on his scooter. "Oh no!" I cried, and we took off. How long had I been in the house?

Jenner needed little encouragement to run. Greyhounds can reach a top speed of forty-five miles per hour, which is why people use them for racing, and Jenner must've been a champion in his day. I was in pretty good shape from volleyball at school, but I could barely keep up with him. Up ahead, Jake was nearing a busier street, and since he had already crossed the two quiet cul-de-sacs that intersected the Andersons' street, I knew he'd have no qualms about crossing the next street. I had to reach him fast.

"Jake!" I screamed. He looked back at me over his shoulder and kept on going. He could be so bad! All I could think about was that my mother was going to kill me. Jake was still halfway up the next block, scootering at full speed. "Jake! Stop!" I cried, louder this time. But he didn't even turn around.

Jenner strained at his leash. Jake was nearing the corner, with only thirty feet to go. Jenner and I crossed the final cul-de-sac—I looked both ways first—and we were only about half a block behind Jake. "Jake!" He looked back one more time and his scooter swerved a little, but he straightened it out and kept going. He was headed right for the busy main street. I froze. Then, in a split second, I just let go of Jenner's leash. He took off at double the speed we'd been running and reached Jake in about fifteen long strides.

Jake was so spooked by the big dog chasing him

19

that he jumped off his scooter sideways, landing with a thud on a soft mound of lawn just before the corner.

I ran as fast as I could and flopped down next to him, gasping, and grabbed his shirt, just in case he hopped back on. Jenner was licking Jake maniacally, and Jake was crying. I grabbed Jenner's collar, too, so I was hanging on to both of them.

"Jenner! Sit!" I said. "Stay," I said firmly, holding my palm out flat toward him. I still had one hand on Jake. "Jakey, are you okay? Are you hurt?" I asked. "Don't cry."

Jake was more scared and mad than anything else. "That doggy tried to bite me!" he accused, pointing a finger at Jenner. Jenner looked at him and whimpered but didn't move.

"Good dog," I said. "Jake, he didn't try to bite you. He saved you! You can't just take off like that. It's dangerous, and dumb, and . . . illegal!" Jake was into law enforcement big-time, so I knew to throw that in.

That got him. Jake stopped crying. "It is not!" he said.

I nodded, knowing I had him now. "Yes. Kids aren't allowed to scooter alone on the sidewalk until they're eight. It's a law."

Jake looked at me skeptically. "I don't believe you."

"Well, it's true. If we see a police officer on the way to Camden's, we can ask. Now come on, let's go. And don't ever take off on me like that again, or I'll have to turn you in at police headquarters." I tried to make my voice sound stern. I didn't even know where the headquarters was.

I picked up Jenner's leash and helped Jake back onto his scooter. I let out a big sigh of relief. Everything was under control again. Jenner stepped off the curb to do his business.

"I still get my candy. Two," said Jake stubbornly. It wasn't a question but rather a statement.

"Well . . . ," I said. Mom was always talking about not rewarding bad behavior. And Jake was definitely bad, taking off like that.

Jake's lower lip began to tremble. "You said!" he accused.

I knew I was in rough territory, but suddenly I was mad too. "Well, that was before you took off, mister!" I said. The aroma of Jenner's business at the curb was unpleasant. I fished in my pocket for the Baggies clip.

"I hate you!" accused Jake.

I sighed and bent to pick up Jenner's poop,

standing on his leash so he didn't wander away. Jake was being a pain and now I had yucky dog doo. Nothing was going according to plan. It couldn't get worse. But as I stood up, I found myself face-to-face with Sydney Whitman, neighborhood resident, founder and president of the Popular Girls Club, and all-around mean girl, and her hench-lady Bella. *Well,* I thought, *I guess my day can get worse.*

I never ran into Sydney except at the worst possible moments. Weeks could go by without seeing Sydney. Then I'd go outside to get the mail in my pajamas on a Saturday and she would walk by, saying, "Oh, Emma, are you sick?" I really didn't like her. I looked at Jenner's poop bag and Jake's tear-streaked face, and my heart sank.

"Pee-yoo!" said Sydney, waving her hand in front of her nose. "Is that the kid's or the dog's?" she asked, giggling. Bella snickered appreciatively.

I rolled my eyes and said nothing.

"I didn't know you had a dog," said Sydney, tossing her long, Barbie-blond hair from one shoulder to the other in a pointless way.

"He's our neighbors'," I said. It wasn't like Sydney knew anything about me, so why should she act like she did?

"Oh good, because he's so ugly, I was going to

feel sorry for you. But I guess I just feel sorry for your neighbors!" She laughed a kind of fake laughter, and Bella joined her.

Poor Jenner, I thought. Greyhounds were funny-looking, but Jenner was a good dog, and he had just saved my little brother. "He's a good dog, aren't you, puppy?" I reached down and gave Jenner a loyal pat, and he licked my hand.

"Gross. I hope you wash that hand before you make cupcakes," said Sydney.

"Yeah!" agreed Bella unoriginally.

Jake stood up. "I hope you wash your face before I take you down to headquarters!" he said loudly, his hands on his hips and his scooter resting at his side. I laughed.

Sydney and Bella turned to look at him. "Isn't he cute?" said Sydney in a sweet voice.

"What's your name, little boy?" asked Bella.

Jake puffed up his chest and refused to answer. *Good boy,* I thought. He might be a pain, but he's my brother. "That's Jake," I said, trying to sound light and breezy. "And he has a date at the candy store. Let's go, buddy." Then I turned my back on Sydney and Bella and lifted Jenner's leash out from under my shoe.

"So long!" said Sydney.

"Later," I said. *Like, much later.*

Bella and Sydney continued walking along the sidewalk, and we headed off to cross the street.

"Thanks for sticking up for me, Jake," I said after a minute.

"Two pieces, right?" said Jake, grinning. Well, the kid was smart. I started laughing.

"Right," I agreed. "Two pieces for you!" Little brothers were a pain, but sometimes they weren't too bad.

CHAPTER 3

Home, Not-So-Sweet Home

After we went to Camden's we took a good long scooter ride around the neighborhood, and Jenner got an extra-long walk. Jake had eaten one Air-Heads and saved another for later. Jenner was tired out and, after a long drink of water, went straight to his doggy bed in the Andersons' kitchen and curled up for a nap. Mrs. Anderson had left an envelope marked "Emma" on the kitchen island, and I picked it up and opened it, then smiled at the five-dollar bill inside and left, closing the door behind me to lock it.

At home Jake went right for the TV, and I grabbed my backpack and flute case to head upstairs to my room. I never really had a problem getting my work done and my flute practice in each day. It was all a matter of scheduling and maximizing my time. I loved making schedules. It felt good to be able to check things off. Plus I liked knowing exactly what was happening when. That way there were no surprises. I hate surprises more than anything. They make me nervous.

After a while I heard my older brother Sam come home from basketball practice, so I went downstairs and found him wolfing down a chicken Parmesan sub at the kitchen sink. He worked nights at the movie theater and didn't usually have time to eat with us.

"Hey, Sam," I said.

"Hey, kiddo," he said. He wiped his mouth with a paper towel and took another bite.

Sam was handsome. There was no denying it. Girls called the house all the time and hung up, giggling, when I answered. I usually just rolled my eyes. It didn't really bother me that they called, but it bothered me that Sam seemed to like it. I can't explain why. I guess I should just get used to it because all my friends have huge crushes on him. Besides being handsome, he was also pretty nice. At least as far as brothers go. He was just so busy between schoolwork (he had to make honor roll to get a scholarship to a Division One college); playing varsity football, basketball, and lacrosse; and his job at the movie theater that he was kind of like a ghost in our family. You'd see signs that he'd been home—a dirty plate, a small pile of laundry on top of the machine—but rarely spy the actual Sam. I was glad to see him.

"What's new?" I asked, reaching for a cookie. Before I could grab it, though, I went to the sink to wash my hands. I couldn't help thinking about Sydney and her dog poo comment.

Sam stepped aside and took a long drink straight from the quart of milk on the counter. "Gross," I said. It was kind of automatic. Honestly, my brothers do so many gross things, I should be used to it by now.

He tipped back the container and finished it. "Mom texted me to say she got taco stuff for you guys. It's in the fridge."

"Okay," I said. At least tacos were easy. I could make them if my dad didn't get home in time. He was trying to leave work earlier now that Mom had to work evenings, but he didn't always make it out early enough to make dinner. Usually Jake and Matt were so hungry and whiny that I ended up making it.

"Anything good on this week?" I asked hopefully.

Sam's job at the movie theater meant sometimes he could get me discounts.

"New Will Smith coming. I can get you half-price passes," he offered. "Four good?"

I smiled, thinking of Mia, Alexis, and Katie. And saving money. "Perfect. Thanks," I said.

"Got any cupcakes in exchange?" asked Sam.

I shook my head sadly. In a house with three boys, cupcakes went fast. "All out. Sorry. I'll make more tomorrow. I promise I'll save you one." I started to go back upstairs. "Have fun at work!" I called.

"Always do," said Sam, and he burped a long, loud belch.

"Gross," I said. Automatic again. There is seriously a lot of burping in my house. "But impressive. Maybe you can get on varsity burping."

I flopped down into the fluffy armchair in my room. I pulled out my music stand, flipped open to the piece I was working on, opened the flute case, and just sat for a minute with my flute in two pieces in my lap. I love my room. It's pink, first off, which is my favorite color. Right before I started middle school my mom told me that we could redo it so it wasn't so babyish. I was really glad to get rid of the Barbie sheets, since I was embarrassed every time I had a friend over. My mom and I worked really hard to get it just right. We went through all these magazines to find just the right look. It took months and months.

We bought a wooden bedroom set—a desk, twin bed with a trundle, a dresser with a tilting mirror on top, and a bedside table—at a yard sale and spray painted it a shiny pale pink. Then we took an old armchair from my grandmother's attic, and Mom had it reupholstered with white fabric that has a pattern of tiny, pale- and hot-pink flowers with green stems so it looked so pretty.

The pièces de résistance, as my mom calls them (which kind of means the "big deal"), are the walls. We copied a project we had seen on a TV design show where they'd covered the walls in panels of fabric with this kind of foam behind it, so now my room is totally cushy, soundproof, and quiet. It's like my own little nest.

After a half hour of practice I dashed off a quick e-mail to the club, asking if anyone wanted to go see the new Will Smith movie on Friday night, and then I cracked open my book bag to start my homework. But the computer called to me again, and I gave in. Just one quick peek, I told myself. I logged on to the Williams-Sonoma website, and there it was. The pale pink KitchenAid mixer. All $250 of it.

I thought about how much faster and easier it would be to turn out delicious cupcakes if I had that mixer. Not to mention breads, muffins, cookies, and more. And I knew I would get a jolt of happiness every time I saw it on the counter. It was that pretty. I pulled open the bottom drawer of my desk and took out the dustcover I'd already bought for the mixer on eBay. It had a pink quilted background with a pattern of cupcakes repeating across it—red velvet, white buttercream, and double chocolate with a cherry on top. I hadn't been able to resist it and only twenty-three dollars, it had been easy to hand the cash over to Mom and convince her to charge it, even though I didn't yet have the machine it would cover. Dad would have refused, being the more practical of the two parents, but my mom understood the importance of dreaming big. She even bought it for me in the end and wouldn't take the dog-walking money I gave her. *One day,* I thought, *that mixer will be mine.*

Just then, there was a knock on the door. "Emma!" came Jake's muffled voice. All the boys knew they had to knock on my door. It was a girls-only zone. Luckily my parents strongly enforced the rule.

"Come in!" I called, and Jake opened the door.

"I'm hungry," he said.

I looked at my watch. Six thirty. "Is Dad home?"

Jake shook his head. I looked at my pile of homework and sighed. Well, I had to eat too.

"Let's go, officer," I said. "I'll make some tacos, okay?"

Jake nodded happily and skipped down to the kitchen.

Tacos are really easy. My mom taught us all how to make them, but I make the least mess in the kitchen, so I try to get there before Matt or Sam does. The family rule is that whoever doesn't cook helps clean up, and if my brothers are in the kitchen, the cleanup goes to a whole other level. I sautéed the ground beef and set out the condiments while Jake set the table (that's his job, and he's okay at it as long as you remind him that you need forks and knives and not just spoons). Matt rolled in midway through and I told him he was on cleanup duty. He nodded. He'd bailed on babysitting Jake today, so he owed me, big-time. He ran up to shower while I finished the cooking.

"Hello, everybody!" Dad's voice echoed through the front hall, and the door clunked shut behind him. I heard his keys drop on the tray on the console. Sam had left, Matt was in the shower, and a bomb couldn't take Jake's interest from the TV.

"Hey, Dad!" I called in reply. "I'm in here!"

Dad walked in, loosening his tie. He was tall and athletic, like Sam, with the same curly hair and the same twinkly blue eyes. He worked at a bank downtown so he had to wear a suit, but to me it always looked like a costume. He looked most like himself when he was in sweats and a T-shirt with a whistle around his neck. He'd coached many of our teams over the years and also played in a men's soccer league at night once a week with his friends.

"Hi, honey!" Dad crossed the kitchen to hug me, and he lifted me up and spun me once, then kissed the top of my head. I knew I was getting a little big for it, but that's what he always did when he came home. At least he'd stopped saying "Hello, my little princess."

Dad sniffed, looked around, then looked relieved. "Thanks for making dinner. You're a star."

I shrugged. "Gotta eat," I said, but I smiled. My parents could depend on me. They always told me that, and I never wanted to disappoint them. Anyway, I liked doing things myself.

Dad rolled up his sleeves and washed his hands in the sink. Then he grabbed a bag of chips and a bowl and some salsa. "I had hoped to get out early so you wouldn't get stuck with dinner, but we had a couple of new deals to process, and I couldn't leave," he said. "How was your day?"

I thought back to school, then the Cupcake Club meeting. "Oh! Mia's mom asked us to be in her wedding!" I said. It was exciting, even if it might be too expensive.

"Wow!" said Dad, reaching for a chip. "That's neat. What do you have to do?"

"We're going to be junior bridesmaids. Actually, I'm not sure what we have to do!" I laughed. It had all been about the dresses, not the actual responsibilities. "I'd better find out."

"You probably just walk down the aisle ahead of the bride. You just have to make sure you smile," said Dad. "That shouldn't be too hard for you." He winked. I was just relieved that he was so clueless about clothes and weddings that he didn't think to ask what we would need to wear; that kind of stuff just wasn't on his radar unless someone spelled it out for him. I wasn't going to tell him about the dress.

"What else happened today?" he asked.

I thought over the rest of the day and decided not to say anything about Matt leaving me with Jake or

Jenner saving Jake's life. But gosh, was it hard to keep what felt like secrets from Dad. I wasn't used to it. Changing the subject was easier. "Hey, can I go to the movies with the Cupcake Club girls on Friday night? Sam's getting us passes."

"Sure," said Dad. Then he started to talk about carpools, and I kind of tuned him out and finished making the tacos. Matt and Jake came in and we all sat down at the table to eat. Except Sam. And Mom of course.

"A doggy saved my life today," said Jake out of nowhere. I felt my face get really red.

"Oh, ha-ha, Jakey. You're such an exaggerator!" I said, laughing a fake laugh.

Dad's eyebrows lifted. "Really. That's pretty interesting. What happened?"

"Well, I was going superfast on my scooter—"

"Hang on, back up," I interrupted. If the story was going to be told, all the details needed to be in place. "I had to walk the Andersons' dog, Jenner, after school, and Mr. Disorganized"—I gestured at Matt—"bailed on Jake because he had practice all of a sudden, so I had to take Jake."

Matt burst in, taco pieces spraying out of his full mouth. "Hey! It's not my fault! The coach changed it last minute, and I called Mom and she said to ask

Emma! I can't miss that stuff, or I'll get benched!"

"Matthew, don't talk with your mouth full. And while you're at it, get your elbows off the table." Dad looked irritated. "Is it true that you bagged Jake today?" he asked.

I smirked at Matt and he gave me a dark look. "Yes, but . . ."

"But what if Emma hadn't come home?" asked Dad.

"Well, obviously I wouldn't have gone and left Jake. I waited until she got here, anyway," said Matt.

Dad sighed. "Listen, guys, the logistics of your mom's new job are tricky, there's no denying it. Three to nine are hard hours for anyone and I know it puts a lot of responsibility on you guys. But we're a family. And families chip in and help out and look out for one another." He looked around the table.

Jake was drooping in his chair. It was past his official bedtime of seven thirty. Matt looked miffed. I tried not to look upset. I missed Mom. It was so much easier when she was here and Matt and I didn't have to babysit every day. I knew it wasn't Mom's fault that she'd been "downsized," or whatever they called it, from her job at the library. And I knew Mom wasn't thrilled about working at the bookstore at the mall. Sure, the discounts were great, but the hours stank and she was on her feet all day for not that much money.

"Here's the deal. If you can't babysit on your assigned day," Dad said, looking at us in that Dad-like way, "then you have to let the other person know as soon as possible. And you owe that person a day. It has to be even. Do you understand?"

We nodded.

"Can I go to bed?" asked Jake.

"Run on up, take off your clothes, and get out your PJs, and I'll come run your shower in one minute," said Dad. Jake scraped back his chair and took off.

"Clear your plate!" I called, but Jake was gone. I turned to Matt. "Okay, you owe me, so you have Friday."

"What? No way!" protested Matt. "I have plans!"

"Me too, and you owe me a day. I can stay with him until five. After that, just take Jake with you," I said. "That's what I did."

"What was all that business about Jake and the 'doggy,' anyway?" asked Dad.

Oh no. "Oh, I had to walk the Andersons' dog, Jenner, and Jake was, uh, going too fast on his scooter, and Jenner, um, stopped him for me," I said. I really did hate to lie. But it was either that or not be able to dog walk on the days I had Jake, and I couldn't afford to lose any jobs.

Dad gave me another look. "Just make sure that Jake is your number one priority when he's with you, okay?" he said sternly, but not really like he was mad.

I nodded.

"And you, too, buddy," he said to Matt. "I'm going up to start Jake's shower and get him to bed. If you can get your dishes in the sink and make a quick plate for Mom, I'll come back down and clean up, okay?"

Matt smiled a gloating smile that he was off the hook for cleanup. I rolled my eyes at him as we all stood up.

"And kids?"

We looked at him.

"Thanks. Thanks for pitching in. You're great kids." He smiled a tired smile and started to leave the kitchen. "I'll have a chat with Mom when she gets home tonight, and we'll work out a better schedule, okay?"

We nodded at Dad and then turned and gave each other dirty looks. The battle was over, but not the war.

CHAPTER 4

Burned

I was so busy with school, flute, babysitting Jake, and walking Jenner that the week flew by. Alexis had sent around our cupcake proposals for approval by e-mail, and after reaching a consensus, she had e-mailed them on to our clients (Mia's mom being one). Friday came quickly, and after a quick pit stop at the grocery store for supplies after school, the Cupcake Club came over for a meeting and to bake up a few samples of a new recipe of Katie's. The plan was that after we baked we would head downtown for a slice of pizza and the movie.

Alexis called the meeting to order and said that Mia's mom would like to sample the bacon cupcakes for the groom's cake before she placed her final order for the wedding cupcakes. Alexis coughed and shot me a look. "She'll love it once she tastes it!" I promised.

We agreed to meet next Friday to bake them; Mia would take them home afterward. Next Mia confirmed the timing for the club's outing to the bridal store the next morning. My stomach turned over as the reality of the dress set in. I hadn't really paid attention to the e-mails about the plan because I didn't want to. I still didn't want to ask Mom for money for it, and I wasn't sure I was going to have enough from dog walking or cupcake making. Finally, we discussed some leads we had for other jobs. Then it was time to bake.

On the menu today were raspberry swirl cupcakes with a pink cream cheese frosting. I was beating the frosting with a hand mixer, having to pause and rest the mixer on its back while I added ingredients. I couldn't help fantasizing about the hands-free pink stand mixer. Someday. Soon!

Mia had brought three bridal magazines, and the others were all flipping through them while the cupcakes baked in the oven. Tomorrow we were going to The Special Day bridal shop at the Chamber Street Mall, and Mia wanted us to get some ideas before we went.

"Here's a really cute one!" declared Katie. I

peered over Katie's shoulder to see the dress she was pointing at. I looked at the price first. All the prices were a lot more than I thought. I had never really paid attention when I went shopping with Mom before, and lately there hadn't been much shopping. I couldn't remember how much a dress was supposed to cost, but the ones in the magazines were a lot of money.

"Ooh! Look at this one!" said Alexis. She handed the magazine across the room to Mia, and I leaned over to see it. It was a white, shin-length dress with a sash. It was beautiful. It was also $350! I gulped and prayed Mia wouldn't like it.

"Oh, that is pretty!" said Mia. "I love it! But three hundred and fifty dollars! No way!"

Whew, I thought. *I love my friends.* "That is crazy!"

"That's business for you, baby," said Alexis, reaching out her hands to take the magazine back. "They want to suck every possible dollar out of the big day."

The back door opened and shut with a bang. "Emma!" It was Sam.

Mia, Alexis, and Katie sat up straight and adjusted their outfits and hair, trying to look good for Sam. It was kind of funny and kind of not. "In here!" I called.

Sam walked into the kitchen. "Yum! Did you save any for me?"

Mia flipped her hair. "We will," she said with a big smile.

"They're not ready yet," I said.

Katie and Alexis stopped talking. And for Alexis that was a big deal. She just looked at Sam and smiled. Katie couldn't even look at him. She stared at her sneakers.

Sam smirked. I think he thought it was cute that all my friends had crushes on him. "Here are your passes for the movie. Have fun!" He slid them across the counter.

"Thanks," I said.

"Have you seen it?" asked Mia.

"Part of it. It's killer," said Sam. "Gotta go!"

The back door opened and slammed closed again.

"He is really cute," said Katie.

"Totally," agreed Mia. "And so nice!"

"Depends on the day," I said. But Sam was pretty nice. Nicer than Matt.

"Such a hard worker . . . ," said Alexis dreamily, and we all roared with laughter. All Alexis thought about was business.

Katie stood and went to peek in the oven at the cupcakes. "Almost," she said.

"Don't overbake them!" warned Alexis, picking up the timer and glancing at it. "Remember our bottom line!"

We'd wasted a whole batch last week because we'd gotten distracted by a reality TV show. We'd had to toss them all and start over; it had been a total waste of money and time.

The phone rang. I checked the caller ID and saw that it was Jenner's owner, Mrs. Anderson, calling from work.

"Hi, Mrs. Anderson," I said. Had I done anything wrong? Mentally I reviewed my last visit to the Andersons'. I was sure I'd locked up.

"Hi, honey. Ooh, that caller ID still gives me a start! Anyway, I was wondering if I could ask a favor?"

"Sure," I said, relieved.

"Any chance you could give Jenner a quick run around the block today? The girls have a birthday party, and I'm going straight from work to meet them there. I totally forgot. The poor guy won't make it. . . ."

I looked at my watch. I had to meet Jake at the school bus in fifteen minutes. The cupcakes would have to come out in a few minutes, then cool before we frosted them. Then we absolutely had to leave for pizza by five, when Matt got home. The movie was at 6:20. But Mrs. Anderson depended on me, and I hated to say no. Plus, if I was going to have to buy a bridesmaid's dress, then I needed the money. I planned it out in my head.

"Hang on just one second while I check something." I covered the phone. "Would you guys meet Jake's bus for me while I run over to the Andersons'?"

The others looked surprised but readily agreed. "Jake's so cute!" said Katie, who didn't have any siblings of her own.

"Let's hope so," I said. Then, returning to the call, I said, "Sure. No problem!"

"Great! I'll just double up on the money for the next time you come, okay?" asked Mrs. Anderson.

"That's fine. Don't worry. Bye!" I hung up and took off my pink apron.

Mia was looking at me strangely.

"What?" I asked. "Mrs. Anderson needs me to walk Jenner. I'll just be a second. The frosting's almost ready. It just needs vanilla and one more whip. Then we'll have to wait until the 'cakes are done to frost them anyway. I'll be back in no time."

"Don't worry! Take your time. It's no problem.

Really." Mia stood to assume the role of chief frosting officer. She smiled, but she seemed . . . well, something was wrong. Was Mia annoyed?

I couldn't think about it long. I had to run. "Okay. Thanks! Be back in less than half an hour. Jake will be here in ten minutes."

I ran down the block to the Andersons'. Jenner jumped up, happy to see me, and I took him out. It took him forever to do his business (probably because he was off schedule), but he finally did, and then I ran him around the block a couple of times for good exercise.

I miscalculated how long that would all take—it had been about forty-five minutes. I glanced at my watch and ran home. When I got there, I saw Jake's backpack flung on the driveway and the back door standing open.

"Hello?" I called, entering the house. But there was no reply. Only the smell of very burnt cupcakes. They were sitting on the counter, dark brown as pretzels and just as hard. "Bummer," I said.

"Guys?" I walked through the downstairs, listening for my friends and little brother. They could hardly be this quiet. I opened the door to the basement rec room. Maybe they were playing video games?

Then I heard a "Hello?" from behind me. It was Matt, just arriving.

I walked back to the kitchen. "Uh . . . are you just getting here?" I asked.

"Yeah, but I'm ten minutes early! Give me a break!" said Matt, bristling. Mom had read him the riot act for ditching Jake on me the other day, and he'd been conscientious about his two turns since then.

"No, no, I'm not annoyed at you. It's just . . ."

"Where's Jake?" asked Matt. My heart sank.

"Uh, I'm not sure."

"Was he here before? I saw his backpack. . . ." Matt headed out to the driveway and I followed him.

"I know, but I had to go walk Jenner . . . so I wasn't here. . . ."

"What?" exploded Matt. "You mean he came home to an empty house?"

"No, my friends were here. I'm sure they met him. I asked them to, but now I don't know where they are."

"You left your friends in charge? Those cupcake girls?" Matt knew that it drove me crazy when he pretended not to know my friends' names.

"Yes, Alexis, Mia, and Katie," I said, trying not

to get angry. "They're very responsible."

"I'm telling Mom!" gloated Matt. "You shirked your duty!"

"Never mind that," I said, starting to get a little panicky. "Where did they go?"

"Well, they couldn't have gotten far. They weren't driving, were they?" he teased.

I didn't answer. He thought it was funny, but I knew something could be wrong. "I'll check the park. Why don't you go check—"

"I'm not checking anything," said Matt happily. "This is your problem. I'll be in here relaxing. Good luck."

"You're a jerk," I said.

I walked quickly to the park, but it still took about five minutes and there was no sign of them there. Where else could they be? The duck pond? I hustled over, but there was no sign of them there either. Oh, why oh why wouldn't my parents let me have a cell phone? (Well, I knew why: It was expensive. Mom and Dad had taken them back as a cost-saving measure. But it was so worth it! I decided to ask for mine back again when Mom got her old job back.)

Ice cream? Camden's? Could they have gone that far? But there was no sign. Now I had been searching for more than twenty minutes, and it was five fifteen. I decided to run home and check to see if they'd returned. By now I realized that my friends would take care of Jake, so nothing bad probably happened. But where were they?

When I turned up my block, I could see that Jake's backpack was no longer in the driveway. And there was certainly no way he'd picked it up himself. One of the girls must have done it. Phew. They were home. I slowed down and sauntered up the driveway, relieved.

But Dad flung open the back door angrily. "Emma! Where is your little brother?"

Oh no! "Isn't he . . . here?" I asked, cringing. Obviously not, since Dad was so mad.

Matt appeared in the doorway behind him, grinning through a mouthful of burnt cupcake.

"I'm going out in the car to look for them," Dad said harshly.

"I'll come," I said readily.

"No, you stay here and call my cell in case they come back while I'm gone." He dashed out and backed the car out of the garage.

"You know these things aren't half bad if you load on the frosting," said Matt as he helped himself to another cupcake.

"Shut up," I said, and went to wait on the back stoop.

Twenty minutes later, which seemed like about four hours later, Jake and the girls returned. I ran in and dialed Dad's cell as soon as I saw them coming. "Good" was all he said, and then hung up. Oh, boy. I ran back outside.

Jake was covered in ice cream, and he held two large candy bars, one in each hand. He was laughing and joking, and the girls were laughing at him. No one seemed hurt or mad or frustrated. Except me.

"What happened?" I demanded, coming down the sidewalk to meet them.

Mia rolled her eyes. "This one sure doesn't like babysitters, do you, pal?" She ruffled Jake's hair.

"I like you!" said Jake winningly. The girls all laughed.

"*Now* you tell us," said Alexis.

"Where were you?" I asked, trying not to yell.

The girls explained how Jake had been upset that I wasn't there to meet him. So he'd had a temper tantrum and taken off down the street. They'd chased him and caught him, at which point he became hysterical and demanded candy.

"He said you buy him two pieces from Camden's

every day!" said Katie incredulously. "Is that true?"

"No, it's not," I said icily. I was glaring at Jake, and he ducked his head guiltily.

"Anyway, we figured we'd better bribe the kid, so we took him around . . ."

"And bought him some stuff," finished Mia.

"Clearly," I said.

"The cupcakes burned while he was having the temper tantrum."

"Luckily, Katie remembered and ran back to turn them off, before they burned down the house."

"That is lucky," I said, thinking that would have really made Dad mad. I looked at my watch. It was 5:40. There was no way we were going to make it for pizza, but we could still make the movie. I was really mad. And really tired. Then I looked up at my friends. They had tried to help me out. It wasn't their fault that Jake was such a pain. I just messed up with the timing. I'd just have to plan better next time, that's all.

"Guys, I'm so sorry. Thank you for dealing. I really appreciate it." I smiled at them. They were such good friends. And I was grateful. "But you!" I said, turning to Jake. "You are in trouble with me, mister! No candy for you next week, not on my watch!"

Jake hung his head. "Okay, sarge," he said.

"Let's go. Matt's waiting for you, and we have to leave. Sorry about the cupcakes, you guys. They were looking good."

"It's okay," said Mia. "How was the dog walking?" she asked.

"Good," I said.

"How much do they pay you?" asked Alexis.

"Five bucks a walk," I said proudly.

"Wow," said Katie. "Pretty good, considering if you had your way, you'd have your own dog and be walking it for free."

I smiled. "Yeah, a dog is definitely not in the budget for our family right now." I felt badly about saying it as soon as it came out of my mouth.

Mia was quiet. We went back to the house and hustled to clean up the kitchen. Then Dad came in.

"Hey, buddy!" he said to Jake as Jake ran to greet him.

"Emma's going to the movies with the babysitters!" said Jake.

"Not yet, she's not," said Dad. "Emma, may I see you in here for a minute, please?"

I felt my face get hot and put down the cupcake tin I was drying. I followed Dad into the living room. I felt my friends' eyes on me.

"Emma," he said quietly. "I know you've got a lot on your plate right now. We all do. But you have taken on way too much. When your brother is in danger because of your decisions, it's time for you to take a look at your priorities. And it sounds like this was the second time this week there was an incident that involved dog walking."

I put my head down, thinking of Jake and Jenner and the scooter ride the other day. "Jake wasn't in danger, though," I protested weakly. I knew Dad was right.

"Your primary responsibilities are to your family and to taking care of yourself. I think it's wonderful that you are so entrepreneurial with the Cupcake Club and the dog walking. I know it's terrific to earn your own money, and . . . well, I know you need it right now for some of the little extras we've cut back on. And I understand that you are trying to incorporate Jake, too, which Mom and I appreciate. But I just think you are getting stretched a little too thin right now. Do you understand?"

I nodded. Visions of expensive bridesmaid dresses swam in my head. Without the cupcakes and the dog walking, there was no way I could afford that dress.

Dad tipped my chin up to look him in the eye.

"You are a very capable young lady. You're just like your mom—organized, energetic, and kind—and we're proud of you. I know Jake can be a handful, but we're all trying to get by the best we can. I just don't want to see you make the wrong decisions or mix up your priorities."

I nodded. I didn't think I was making wrong decisions. I was getting things done. I was walking Jenner and doing my homework and practicing flute and contributing to the Cupcake Club and helping out as much as I could at home. I even made dinner a lot. Jake was the only thing that was a problem. I knew that was mean, but it was true.

Dad sighed. "You're a good kid, sweetheart. And I hate to say this, but if there's another incident with Jake . . . we're going to have to make some hard decisions about what you can and can't spend your time on, okay? And that includes the club and dog walking."

"It's okay, Dad. I understand," I said, but I really didn't. *I would just do better,* I thought. I didn't want anyone to worry about me. And I could take care of myself pretty well.

Dad hugged me and patted me on the head. "Now it's time to go."

"I can still go to the movies?" I said, kind of surprised.

Dad laughed. "Yes, you should go have fun with
your friends."

"Thanks, Dad!" I said, and flung my arms around
him. Then I ran into the kitchen.

Katie, Alexis, and Mia were waiting, having finished cleaning up the whole kitchen.

Matt smirked at me from the TV room, where he
and Jake were watching *SportsCenter*. I could tell he
was happy I was in trouble. And that he thought I
was grounded. "Have fun, kids!" Matt said.

"We will!" I called back with a big smile on my
face.

Matt looked like he couldn't believe it. I felt
good. Things were getting better already.

"The pizza's on me," said Dad, glaring at Matt.
"You still have time, and I'll drop you off."

We all climbed into the minivan and off we went.
I just hoped the Will Smith movie had nothing to
do with cupcakes or dogs. Or brothers.

CHAPTER 5

The Dress That Takes the Cake

Mom was making her specialty—banana chocolate-chip pancakes—for breakfast on Saturday morning. I could smell the bananas and warm, melting chocolate all the way up in my room, even with the door closed. I lay in bed thinking about them until I could taste them. Then I couldn't wait anymore and scrambled downstairs to the kitchen.

"Hi, Mama!" I called, using my babyish, private name for Mom. In public, of course, she was Mom. And in public I was Emma.

"Good morning, lovebug!" Mom said back, using her babyish, private name for me. Mom was already dressed in khakis and a cute lavender sweater. Her blond hair was tied back in a short, bouncy ponytail with a pink ribbon, and she had Keds on her feet. Mom got dressed within five seconds of getting up. I only saw her in her pajamas when she was sick. People always joked that she looked like she could be my sister, but when you got close, you could see from her smile lines that she was definitely mom age.

Mom came around the island to give me a big squeeze and a kiss on top of my bed head. I hopped up on a stool, tucking my legs up under my nightie.

"Yum. Thanks, Mama, for making these."

"I've been craving them myself," Mom said. "But I'm really making them as a thank-you to all you kids. I know what a bumpy week this has been, and I really appreciate all your help. I'm very proud of you all."

I wasn't sure Mom should be too proud of Matt the Brat or Jake the Snake, or even me (Emma the . . . ?), but I didn't say anything. Late last night, when everyone had come home and was relaxing in the TV room (everyone except Jake, who had been fed and bathed and put to bed at a reasonable hour by Mom), everyone agreed that Mondays and Wednesdays were Matt's days to meet Jake, and Tuesdays and Thursdays were mine. Sam would meet him on Fridays. Everyone was happy with the solution for now, and there was a temporary peace in our house.

"So how's your new job?" I asked, propping my chin in my hand. "Give me all the deets."

Mom started filling me in on all the details of the characters she worked with, and the sections of the store that she managed (cooking and fiction), and where she went on her breaks. She told me that she saw a few cookbooks that had some cupcake recipes I might like. It felt good to just be relaxing in the kitchen. I wasn't worried about babysitting Jake or walking Jenner or how much things cost. I was just happy to be with my mom, eating pancakes. It was like it used to be.

"So today's the day I'm going to the mall with Mia and her mom and all the CC girls to look for the dress," I said. I wasn't sure where I was headed with this. I had filled Mom in on the exciting junior bridesmaid news already.

"Ooh! What fun!" said Mom. She was quiet for a moment, then she bit her lip. She had that worried look on her face that she seemed to get a lot these days.

"What?" I asked, but I already pretty much knew.

"Oh, nothing. I was just thinking," said Mom.

"Are you wondering how much the dress will cost?" I asked quietly. "Because I have . . ." I gulped. "I have money saved up that I can use."

"Oh no, sweetheart. It isn't that at all! Really. And I don't want you to use your savings on something like that. Not when you've worked so hard. That's for the mixer! Look, we'll just cross that bridge when we come to it, okay? You just find a pretty dress today, and then Dad and I will figure it out."

But what if I found a dress that was too expensive? I was worried. I guess I'm a lot like Mom because the same worried look must have showed on my face. Mom wiped her hands on the worn apron she was wearing and then leaned over, putting her arms around me.

"I love you, muffin, and I don't want to see you taking the weight of the world on your shoulders. Dad and I can make things work. Okay? It's not all up to you. Though I appreciate your sensitivity and your work ethic, the most important thing is that you have fun at the store today and on the wedding day. The rest will fall into place, all right?"

I smiled to make her feel better, but I felt awful. I hated seeing Mom so worried. And all for a silly dress. I would just pay for the dress myself. I'd take my cupcake and dog-walking money and use my mixer-fund money to pay for the rest. The mixer could wait. It wasn't that bad to use the handheld one. I felt a lot better.

Mom turned back to the stove and loaded up another plate of gooey, sweet pancakes. "Hot off the press!" she said. "Enjoy!" and she handed it to me.

"Yum!"

"Now let's talk about your trip to the bridal store today! What fun!" Mom said. "What color dress do you think you'll buy?" Mom was excited and suddenly I was too. And we talked about colors and long or short dresses and sashes and bows, and I finished a third plate of pancakes before Matt came downstairs and yelled, "Hey, save some for me!" and Mom got up to get him some too.

The ride to the mall was giggly. We were squished into Mia's mom's Mini Cooper, but we didn't mind. But because of the tight space and the squishing and the fact that we were really excited, we couldn't stop laughing. Sometimes that happens a lot with us, and we just laugh so hard that we can't stop.

"What did you cupcake girls eat for breakfast today? Frosting?" asked Mia's mom with a grin, and this made us all laugh harder. We finally got it together as we walked through the mall and into the store.

The Special Day bridal store made us all quiet. There was a big white door and as soon as you stepped inside, it was like another world. There was thick, plush white carpeting and big white sofas and chairs and pretty roses all over the store, in big pots, in vases, and even hanging from a gleaming chandelier. Everything was quiet, and there was soft music playing. It was the prettiest store I had ever seen.

"Isn't it incredible?" Mia whispered to me.

"To die for!" I said, using one of Mom's favorite expressions. And it was.

"Like a fairy tale," Katie said breathlessly.

"Is this a franchise?" asked Alexis, looking around. I rolled my eyes and laughed. Alexis didn't have a romantic bone in her body.

Inside, the tall, elegant manager came to the front of the store to meet us with her hands out-stretched in a friendly greeting. "Call me Mona," she declared. She kissed Mia's mom on each cheek, and then Mia's mom took a moment to properly introduce each of us. Mona made a special effort to greet each of us, complimenting our looks or outfit and saying how happy she was to have us in her store. I wasn't used to salespeople being so nice. Usually they just rang me up or opened the dressing room door with one of those little keys.

"Follow me, ladies," said Mona. "Let's go back where we can be comfortable and talk about what you are looking for."

"Wow," whispered Katie as we followed Mona's trim, stylish figure across the white wall-to-wall carpeting. "This is superfancy."

I got a little nervous. It was fancy. And fancy meant expensive.

There were gorgeous wedding dresses on mannequins and on racks on the walls, and more beautiful chairs and sofas and coffee tables with Kleenex boxes and oversize white binders that Mia pointed out as "look books." Because they'd been here before to select her mom's dress, and because her mom worked in fashion, Mia was very comfortable in the fancy setting. I noticed that all the salespeople were really pretty (prettier than most of the customers, which was kind of funny) and everyone spoke in hushed and ladylike tones. Like "indoor voice," as we told Jake. I stood up straighter, and I was glad I'd taken Mom's advice and dressed up for the occasion in a skirt and my ballet flats. This was not the kind of place to wear sneakers.

We settled into sofas and chairs around a table. There was a plate piled high with delicate sugar cookies, and there was a silver tea service. My grandmother had a tea set like that, but I had never seen her actually use it. I noticed there were a lot of tissue boxes around. I pointed at them.

"Oh," said Mia, "that's because the brides are so beautiful, everyone cries a lot."

Mona assigned one assistant to dole out snacks to us, and another was sent to round up the rack of junior bridesmaid dresses. I noticed there was an entire row of mirrors so you could see yourself in all directions.

Mona's assistant handed me two cookies and tea, and it was a little weird to eat while I was staring at myself in all the mirrors. Mia was so excited, she was jumping around. She went to help her mom put her dress on in the changing room and the three of us were left alone for a moment.

"Can you believe this?" whispered Katie.

"I'm never leaving," I said, nibbling on a cookie.

"Hey, I wonder where they buy these cookies?" said Alexis, inspecting hers as if it would have a label on it. "We should ask Mona if they'd like us to supply them with cupcake minis—white cake with white frosting, of course."

I laughed. "Look out, Bill Gates, there's a new mogul in town."

"Seriously," said Alexis.

"Actually, it's brilliant," I said. "Why don't you ask her? I would totally love to bake for her. Maybe we can drop off some samples for her next week?" All I could think of was coming back again.

"What's up with the Kleenex everywhere?" asked Katie.

"I noticed that too!" I said. "Mia said it's because brides make people cry."

Alexis grabbed a Kleenex and pretended to mop her eyes. "Oh, honey, you've never looked so lovely!" she said dramatically. Sometimes Alexis could be really funny.

The dress assistant came back with a cart laden with white dresses that hung in plastic protective covers.

Then Mona came out and smiled as she watched us ooh and aah over the dresses. "Why don't you each select two to try on, and then we can have a fashion show?" she suggested.

We didn't need to be told twice. Katie went first, then Alexis. It was like playing "Princess for a Day." Mona watched and laughed and clapped.

While Alexis and Katie tried on their dresses, I

tried to poke around on the rack to see if any had price tags on them, but none of them did. I started to worry again. Then I just chose the two plainest dresses I could find and sat down and waited my turn.

While I waited, I picked up one of the look books that Mona had laid out for us. Mia explained that a look book was like a catalog. This one looked like a photo album, but all the pictures were dresses. It was filled with one beautiful dress after the other. Alexis and Katie came to peer over my shoulders.

Suddenly I stopped flipping. In front of me was the prettiest dress I'd ever seen, excluding actual wedding dresses, of course. It was white and the top was a fitted, T-shirt kind of cut with short, puffy sleeves. It had pleats cascading down that were tulle. I knew it was tulle because it was the same material as the long tulle tutu Mom made me one year for a recital. It looked like a fairy princess dress.

"Wow," I said. "This is beautiful." My heart actually fluttered; it was that great.

"I love it!" declared Katie.

"Love what?" asked Mia, coming out from her mom's changing room.

Alexis smiled. "Emma has found our dress," said Alexis.

"Let's see!" said Mia eagerly. She rushed over. "No way," she said solemnly. "I don't believe it."

She stood up and flung her arm out toward her mom's door.

"What?" I asked.

"Here comes the bride!" sang Mia's mom, emerging from the changing room.

I gasped. Ms. Vélaz's dress was a nearly identical but grown-up version of the dress I had just found. It was like they were meant to be together. For a second I forgot about our dresses, though, because Ms. Vélaz looked so beautiful. Her dress was strapless, and her hair was pulled back. She looked really glamorous and not like a mom at all.

"Wow!" was really all I could say.

"Oh, Ms. Vélaz! You look like a . . . a . . . ," cried Katie, suddenly speechless. Alexis nodded in mute agreement.

"A princess!" I said. And it was true.

Ms. Vélaz laughed. "I do just love it. It's the prettiest dress I've ever worn."

"And it looks just like the dress Emma found in the book for us!" declared Mia.

"Oh . . ." I was embarrassed. I didn't mean to pick out everyone's dress for them. Plus, if it was like Ms. Vélaz's dress, then it was probably really expensive.

"Great!" said Ms. Vélaz. "I can't wait to see it! Let me just get this pinned and I'll come look."

Mona swooped over, her mouth filled with straight pins, and while Ms. Vélaz stood on a carpet-covered box, Mona began nipping and shortening, muttering, "Divine, just divine."

"It's divine," whispered Alexis, in a high voice. I tried not to laugh.

"Mona, I think the girls found another dress to try on," said Ms. Vélaz, watching in the mirror as Mona worked.

"Patricia, please go look," said Mona around a mouthful of pins. I wondered how she could talk like that. Patricia came over, and I pointed to the dress. Suddenly I hoped they didn't have it. Or that at least it was very cheap. Or on sale. Oh no! What if it was a fortune?

"Oh yes, the Jumandra. So pretty. That might be in the shipment that came in this morning," said Patricia. "Let me go look."

My heart sank. *Please let it be cheap. Please let it be cheap,* I repeated like a mantra in my head as Patricia flipped through the rack of dresses.

"Here it is!" said Patricia. She plucked it from the rack and whipped the clear plastic cover off of it.

My heart fluttered again when I saw the dress. It

65

was even prettier in real life! But I didn't want to get my hopes up. And the decision wasn't up to me anyway. But Katie, Mia, and Alexis all started yelling, "That's it! That's it!"

"You go try it on first since you found it!" said Mia generously.

"No, no," I waved my hand. "You go first. Or maybe you don't even want to try it . . . that's fine!" I felt like a dork.

"Honey, Mia has tried on dozens of dresses already between her two visits here. You run and put it on. I know it will look lovely on you," said Mia's mom. "Go on . . . Patricia will help you."

"Well . . ."

"Go!" commanded Alexis, and I was up off the couch like a shot, and into the changing room, practically ripping my skirt and sweater off in excitement. Patricia came in with me, which was a little embarrassing, but I just pretended that she was Mom.

As I was standing in my undies, Patricia carefully removed the delicate dress from its padded satin hanger, then cautiously she lowered it over my head. I poked my arms through, and Patricia buttoned me up. Then she gave me a pair of fancy satin shoes to slip on.

"Oh my gosh," I whispered as I saw myself in the mirror.

"Your hair might look pretty down," said Patricia. I pulled out my ponytail and shook my head. She was right. I felt like a fairy. Or a princess. Or a ballerina. Or all of them. It was a dreamy dress. A dream dress.

"Come out!" called Mia.

"How does it look?" called Alexis.

I almost didn't want to go out there. *Maybe,* I thought, *just maybe it wasn't too much. But it had to be expensive.*

"It looks terrible!" I joked through the door.

"What?" cried Katie in alarm.

"Kidding!" I said. I spun around again.

"Ready?" Patricia grinned at me.

And then, oh, what the heck, I nodded yes, and Patricia flung open the door.

"Oh my God!" said the Cupcake Club in unison.

"Oh my God!" said Mia's mom.

CHAPTER 6

The Dream Dress

I felt like everyone came at me at once. Mia's mom came bounding down from her pedestal, Mona and pins in tow. Patricia and the other assistant clustered around me, and they were all chattering at once.

"Oh, Mommy, this is it! Isn't it?" cried Mia ecstatically.

"It's glorious, and it looks spectacular on you, darling," said Ms. Vélaz.

"Divine, just divine," uttered Mona. (*Did she know any other adjectives?* I wondered.) Alexis giggled again.

"Come here, sweetie," said Mona. I climbed up on the box in front of the mirror, and Mona started pinning the dress on me. She fluffed my hair, fluffed the dress, and then stood back.

"Perfect," said Ms. Vélaz.

I could not stop smiling. I was so happy. It was the most beautiful dress I had ever seen, and it was the most beautiful I had ever felt. "It's pretty great," I said quietly. Then I remembered it was really more Mia's day than mine. After all, it was her mom who was getting married. "Mia, why don't you try it on?"

"Okay, but take one more minute. It looks so incredible on you," said Mia generously.

Ms. Vélaz had disappeared and returned with her phone. "Let me take a photo and send it to your mom," she said happily. "You look so fabulous."

I didn't think fast enough and the picture was snapped. Mia's mom's fingers flew over her keyboard writing the message to Mom. "What's her e-mail address again?" asked Ms. Vélaz. I panicked. Now Mom would see the dress and know we'd found something for sure. She would ask Ms. Vélaz how much it cost. I had to think.

"Umm . . . I don't know what her new one is since she switched jobs," I said in relief, realizing it was true. "Why don't you just send it to me, and I'll show it to her when I get home?"

Ms. Vélaz glanced at me, then took down my

e-mail address and pushed send as Mona returned to the room. The two of them stepped off to chat quietly, and Patricia led me back to the dressing room.

As I passed Mona and Ms. Vélaz, I heard the words "two hundred and fifty dollars." I felt sick.

Two hundred and fifty dollars!

This was way, way worse than I had imagined. *Okay,* I thought. *If they pick this dress for sure, I'll just excuse myself from being a junior bridesmaid.* It was crazy beautiful, but whole families (mine!) could be fed for weeks for that kind of money. Dream dress indeed. I could dream about it, but I would never be able to afford it. "Good-bye, beautiful," I whispered to the dress on its satin hanger.

I sat on the couch in a daze as one by one, all the girls tried it on and fell in love. It looked slightly different but equally amazing on all of us, just like the jeans in *The Sisterhood of the Traveling Pants*, I thought distractedly. By the time everyone had it on, the decision had been made. This was the dress. *Oh no,* I thought. *What have I done?*

Ms. Vélaz whispered to Mona about the dresses a little more. She turned to us. "Girls, is this okay with all of you? Are you sure your parents will be okay with this dress?"

Katie and Alexis nodded. "My mom is just happy I'll be in a dress," said Alexis, who almost always wore pants. For a second I was jealous of my friends. None of them seemed worried about spending $250 on a dress. They were acting like it was no big deal. I noticed Mia's mom looking at me with a worried look. I started to sweat a little. I smiled, as if I was agreeing.

"Well, that's the dress then!" said Ms. Vélaz. Then it was decided that the four of us ought to go put the dresses on hold up at the front desk, and we'd each come back with our parents to buy it. "If there's a problem, just let me know," said Ms. Vélaz. Mona nodded. I sighed with relief. On hold was different than sold. I might be able to figure something out.

The Cupcake Club followed Patricia the assistant out of the room and cruised soundlessly across the plush carpet to the front counter to fill out the paperwork. The store had filled up quite a bit, and there were groups of women and girls arranged all around in little seating clusters. Suddenly I spied a familiar shock of long blond Barbie hair. Sydney Whitman!

"Guys," I said quietly to warn them, but it was too late. Sydney had seen us.

"Oh my God! Mia!" she squealed, and she jumped up and pranced over to Mia, as if they were the best of friends. "What are you doing here?" she asked excitedly, completely ignoring the three of us.

Katie and Alexis stood frozen, like deer in headlights. Sydney ignored me so I tried to ignore her. Mia did the talking.

"My mom's getting married and we're all in the wedding, so we're getting our dresses. What are you doing here?" Mia was pleasant but cool.

"My cousin Brandi is getting married, and I'm the maid of honor," bragged Sydney.

"Wow," said Mia nicely. She had a hard time being mean.

"So what are you wearing?" asked Sydney, looking Mia over from head to toe.

Mia fielded the question again. "Oh, we found a gorgeous dress. It looks great on everyone. Especially Emma. Actually, she was the one who found it."

Sydney looked at me as if she had just realized I was there. Then she looked back at Mia. "Can I see it?"

"Oh, uh . . ." Mia hesitated.

Sydney looked at the counter, where Patricia was

calmly laying out four sets of paperwork and four pens, for us to order three more dresses. The dress was on a hanger, hanging behind the counter.

"Is that it?" cried Sydney. "It is too cute!"

Patricia looked up and smiled. "It looks wonderful on the girls," she said kindly.

Sydney squinted sideways at it, then tilted her head.

"Brandi?" she called over her shoulder. "Brandi? Can you come here for a minute?"

Another very blond, older girl, with lots of makeup and a pink sweat suit, came over to stand by Sydney.

"Cu-uuu-uuute," said Brandi, drawing the word out into three syllables. She snapped her gum. "Try it on, then come show me," she instructed, and she went back to her group on the couch.

"I'll try it too," said Sydney to Patricia.

Patricia looked dubious. "I'll check to see if there's another one in the back," she said diplomatically, then she disappeared.

Probably going to check with Mona on what to do, I thought. I knew it was bad luck for anyone out of the wedding party to know what the bride's dress looked like, but how about the bridesmaids' dresses? Was there a rule about that? *Please let Mona say yes, please let Mona say yes,* I thought fervently. I might not be able to afford it, but the idea of Sydney in my dress made me sick.

Patricia returned with a sympathetic look on her face. "I'm so sorry, miss, but we only have one of these in stock and we can only order a few in each size. We don't like too many of our weddings to look the same. As soon as we finish the paperwork here, I'll be happy to help your bridal consultant find something similar." She smiled and turned away, letting Sydney know the matter was closed. Then she started wrapping up the remaining dress for Mia.

"Wait!" said Sydney, never one to give up. "Mia, do you mind if I try this one? Then, if it looks good, maybe I can order it online or something."

I thought that was a pretty rude thing to say in front of Patricia and also pretty pushy. But Mia was so sweet.

"Uh, sure . . . I guess so." Mia shrugged.

"Great," said Sydney.

Patricia raised her eyebrows at Mia but passed the dress over the counter to Sydney. "Please be careful with it," she said.

"Of course," said Sydney. And she flew off, the dress flapping behind her from its hanger.

Seconds later Sydney returned, beaming, in the dress. Her whole group squealed and clapped as

Sydney twirled, and the Cupcake Club looked on in dismay. It did look amazing on her. It was just that kind of dress, and Sydney was beautiful after all.

"I love it!" Sydney called to Mia. Mia nodded, unsmiling.

Patricia shook her head and went and whispered in Brandi's bridal consultant's ear. The consultant nodded, and then went and spoke to Sydney. It was time for the dress to come off. With some difficulty, she persuaded Sydney to return to the changing room and remove the dress. Moments later it was back on its hanger, safely behind the register.

"Did that really just happen, or was it a nightmare?" asked Katie.

I felt the same way. I looked at her.

"It happened." Katie sighed.

"Sorry, guys," whispered Mia. "I didn't know what else to do."

"You are way too nice," said Alexis. "I would have charged her to try it on."

The Cupcake Club all laughed. "We know you would have!" I said.

Katie, Alexis, and I finished the paperwork and slid it across the counter to Patricia. She looked it over.

"Emma?"

Uh-oh. What now? I bit my lip.

"Can I have a daytime phone number for one of your parents, please?" She smiled encouragingly at me.

"Oh, um. My mom's just started a new job, and I don't know her number, so . . ."

"How about your dad?" asked Patricia.

I felt panicky. "Ugh, I hate to bother him with stuff like this at work. Why don't I . . . have my mom call you with her new number?"

Patricia nodded and handed me a business card. "That would be just fine. In the meantime we can order it for you so its here on time."

It would be fine, I said to myself. I would find the money somehow. It was a dream dress. And I could dream big. I wouldn't worry my parents. I would handle it.

CHAPTER 7

Between a Rock and a Dress

$\mathcal{I}$ spent the weekend counting money and adding numbers. I didn't even want to ask my parents for half the money for the dress, let alone all of it. I needed a plan to get to $250. I'd have to really scrimp on after-school treats, like getting candy for Jake or going to the movies. Then I'd have to up the dog walking and the cupcake making. The only problem was they kind of used the same time slot and the dog walking paid better. *I can do this*, I thought. *I can plan this out. But how?*

I was still thinking about it when I left school on Monday and walked to the bike rack. I was nearly next to Matt before I saw him waiting for me by my bike.

"Hey," he said.

"Hi, yourself," I said, eyeing him suspiciously. "What's up?"

"Well . . . I was wondering if we could trade days. If you could do today, I'll do tomorrow, I swear."

I sighed. I could barely figure out my plans, and they were already getting messed up. I was supposed to go to Katie's today to make cupcakes for Henry Garner's birthday party tomorrow. *I could bring Jake,* I thought. *He couldn't be that bad. Plus, tomorrow was a dog-walking day, so maybe it would be better if he were with Matt then.*

"Fine," I said.

The relief in Matt's face was obvious. "Thank you so much," he said, and he actually seemed to mean it.

"What do you have?" I asked. "Practice?"

"Uh . . ." Matt looked awkward for a second, and then looked a little embarrassed. "You know how I like to fool around on the computer?"

I nodded.

"Well, there's a three-hour intensive workshop for graphic design down at the computer center at the library, and I didn't realize it was today. Don't tell Mom and Dad, though, okay? I'm paying for it with my birthday money from Grandma."

"Cool," I said. I was surprised, though. Not that I really cared what Matt did, but I thought it would be something dumb, like pizza with the guys. I guess he didn't want to ask Mom and Dad for money either. We looked at each other for a second, understanding. "Well, good luck," I said.

"Thanks," said Matt, and he took off.

That was probably the most civilized conversation I've had with him in months, I thought as I pedaled home. I wasn't due to be at Katie's until four thirty so I'd go home, change, get Jake, and head over.

Poor Jake was not psyched about going to Katie's until I reminded him that he could lick the bowl (and the beaters, he insisted), and he could watch Katie's TV.

"What's up, Cupcakers?" I asked, trying to smile brightly as we arrived. "I've brought my apprentice, Officer Jake Taylor, along with me today." Then over his head I mouthed, *Sorry*.

Jake saluted the girls, and while Katie and Alexis giggled, Mia solemnly saluted him back. She was his favorite, and I could see why. Nobody seemed mad at me, so that was good.

Henry Garner was having a circus-themed birthday with a clown, so we'd decided to do clown cupcakes for the party. This meant yellow cake with red-and-white-striped cupcake papers, Froot Loops eyes, a licorice whip smile, red frosting hair, and frosted ice-cream cones as pointy clown hats. I put Jake in charge of sorting Froot Loops by color, and I said he could eat some but not all of them.

Alexis was also making some mini cupcakes that she was bringing over for Mona to sample that evening since we kind of burned the ones from the last Jake episode. Alexis thought Mona might buy them for the store, and I was really excited about that. Maybe it would mean I could go back there again. Plus, it meant more business, and that meant more money.

As usual, we paid for the cost of the supplies out of our treasury; all money received went into it too. It was tricky to price fancier cupcakes, like the clowns, because we had a hard time valuing our labor and time and, after all, we weren't professionals with degrees from culinary schools. But if we covered our costs and made at least a 20 percent profit—what Alexis had determined—for each sale, we were pleased. Actually we were all pretty happy to come out even, but everyone was afraid to tell that to Alexis. Once a month Alexis divided the extra money we had, and we used it to go out for ice cream or pizza to celebrate. After that we each kept what little we had left. I hoped we'd have a little extra this month.

We got right to work measuring, pouring, mixing, and pouring again. The first four trays of cupcakes went into the ovens (Katie's mom had two side by side), and while we waited, I began coloring some of the buttercream frosting a deep red for the Bozo hair.

We were quiet, which seemed a little weird. I looked over at Jake, who was also quiet, and realized why: He had cake batter dripping all down the front of him from licking the spoon and the bowl.

"Oh, Jakey, you need an apron!" I lunged across the kitchen for paper towels and an apron, but all I could find in the apron drawer were large, ruffled, flowery aprons.

"I'm not wearing that stinky girl apron!" Jake was immovable on the subject. "No, sir!" He also refused to take off his shirt.

"Jake, this is gross. And you can't go sit on Katie's mom's couch like that to watch TV."

Mia took over and, while pretending to arrest him and frisk him for weapons, she carefully wiped him clean. I watched in wonder and shook my head. He was like putty in her hands.

We started talking about the wedding. I thought Jake was watching TV but suddenly there was chaos. Jake had gone to remove the electric beaters that I had been using to make the red frosting so he could lick them, and had accidentally turned them on, sending red frosting spattering everywhere, including all over Mia and all over the kitchen.

At first I panicked that he lost a finger or something. When I realized it was all just frosting, I looked at the mess, and I just lost it. "I can't take you anywhere!" I shouted at Jake. "And it's not fair that I have to watch you all the time!" Everyone stopped working and stared at me.

"Shh, Emma, it's okay. We can clean it up," said Katie soothingly.

"I'll take Jake," said Mia, and she and Jake went off to borrow an old T-shirt of Katie's.

Once the tears started, I had a hard time stopping them. I was upset about the mess, upset about having to be in charge of Jake so much, upset that he always ruined everything, and most of all, upset about the dress. It just didn't seem fair. I cried and cried and cried.

"Okay," said Katie, after Mia had returned without Jake, who was now watching *SpongeBob* in the other room. "Emma, we need to talk."

Katie patted a seat at the table next to her, and I sat down, still teary. Alexis and Mia sat across from me. Everyone looked concerned.

"You seem really stressed out," said Katie. Her head was tilted to the side as she looked at me. I don't know why that made me cry more.

"Are you getting enough sleep?" asked Alexis directly. Alexis was a big believer in the basics of life. If you slept well, ate well, and exercised, pretty much everything else would fall into place.

"Not really," I admitted. "I'm pretty busy."

Alexis sat back and folded her arms in satisfaction. "A good night's sleep is so important," she said. She sounded like Mom.

"It seems like you have a lot on your plate," said Mia.

I nodded.

"You have the Cupcake Club. And babysitting. And dog walking. And orchestra. Plus homework. Can we help you?" Alexis asked kindly.

Not to mention saving money, I thought. Then I felt badly. I didn't really want to talk about this with them. What could they do? They would just feel sorry for me, and I didn't want that at all.

"Do you want a break from your responsibilities

with the club?" asked Alexis. "Like a leave of absence?"

I noticed Mia watching me carefully for my response. It gave me a little chill. Did Mia want me out of the club? I thought for a second. I could use the extra time for dog walking and make some money. But if I took a break, it would be like quitting my friends. Plus, I love the club. But if I stayed with it, I'd have to really be present and do a good job—an even better job than in the past because I'd have to prove how committed I really was. I'd have to figure it out. Gee, that seemed to be a theme these days.

Finally I said, "No, but thanks. The Cupcake Club is the best part of my busyness. I'd rather be baking and working and hanging out with you guys than anything else." It was true, after all.

I saw Mia and Katie exchange a glance.

"Well, if it starts to feel like it's too much, just, um, let us know. We won't cut you out of the earnings if you miss a baking session here and there," said Alexis, but I watched her look uneasily at Mia and Katie.

"Thanks, you guys," I said. "You're awesome." But I was really thanking Alexis. There was something going on that I couldn't put my finger on.

Mia and Katie seemed like they didn't believe me, and I wasn't sure they were exactly on board with Alexis. Good old Alexis.

And then, "The cupcakes!" cried Katie.

She leaped to the oven just in the nick of time. They were golden brown and perfect.

The tension was cut for now by our successful batch.

"Phew!" I said, but I wasn't only talking about the cupcakes.

CHAPTER 8

Dog Days

*T*he next day Alexis caught up with me as I was heading to the Andersons' to walk Jenner.

"Hey! I just checked my e-mail, and we have good news!" called Alexis as she came jogging up.

I was running late, but I stopped. "What's up?" I asked.

Alexis grinned. "Mona loved the sample minis!"

"She did?" I cried. I was so excited.

Alexis nodded. "Yup, and she wants to place an order for five dozen every Saturday for the next two months!"

"Oh my God! That is amazing," I said, thinking about the profits. Then I thought about dropping them off at the beautiful store. "What will we charge her?" I asked. "And how will we get them to her?"

Alexis nodded again. "Already thought of all that. The minis are fifty cents each, so that's thirty dollars a week. For eight weeks it's two hundred and forty dollars. My mom said she'll take me to drop them off on the way to soccer every week."

"That is so great! Thanks, Alexis! So we'll bake every Friday night?"

"We kind of already do, anyway," said Alexis. "But yeah. Where are you going? Jenner?"

I nodded. "Yup. I love him and the cool part is, he seems to love me back! He behaves so well for me. Unlike Jake," I added.

Alexis pursed her lips thoughtfully. "You know, you could really make it worth your while if you had more than one dog at a time."

I had already thought of that as part of the dream dress plan. "I know. I just haven't had the time to try to drum up more business."

"Well . . . you just need to maximize your time while you're doing it. So, like, wear a T-shirt that says 'Dog walking, five dollars a walk' with your e-mail address or whatever on it," Alexis said.

"That's a cute idea. I can do that with some fabric markers."

"And you could make a flyer on the computer

and hand it out or put it in mailboxes while you're out walking."

"Oooh! Good one!"

Alexis laughed. "And . . . you could, like, spray liver perfume on you or carry a lot of doggy treats in your pockets, so when you pass a dog on the street it goes crazy for you!"

I laughed too. "I think I'll skip the liver perfume, but thanks. Treats in my pocket is a good idea. I've been meaning to do that. Thanks!"

"Anytime. You know I love brainstorming about marketing," said Alexis with a smile. But then she turned suddenly serious. "Hey, maybe you should put cupcake flyers in the mailboxes too!"

"I could do that," I said. But something about her voice made me nervous.

"Just to, you know, help out a little," said Alexis casually.

I felt a pit in my stomach. "Oh. Am I . . . not helping out enough?"

Alexis looked away uneasily. "No, I mean, I think you are. . . ."

"Do the others think I'm not?" I asked anxiously. Was this what was going on at that last baking session? I missed some meetings, sure. And I brought Jake a few times. But I was trying, I really was.

"No, no, not at all. I think . . . Maybe they're just nervous about all the work we have these days, and they just want to make sure you're committed. You've missed a few baking sessions. And you seem a little preoccupied." Alexis shrugged. "That's all. But don't tell them I told you, okay?"

"Okay," I agreed hesitantly. "Thanks, I guess. . . ."

"Listen, Emma," said Alexis. "I know they might think you're flaking out a little on things. And you don't seem into the dress at all. . . ."

"What?" I cried. I hadn't thought about anything besides that dress!

Alexis cleared her throat. "Your mom told my mom about her job and that it's been a little . . . well . . . a little crazy at your house lately with all the babysitting."

I wondered how much Mom told Mrs. Becker and how much Alexis knew.

"I can help you," Alexis said. "Anytime. Just ask, okay? My mom's never home after school either." Alexis smiled. It was true, Mrs. and Mr. Becker got home really late, and a lot of times Alexis just ate dinner with her sister. My mom used to invite them over a lot for dinner, but I realized she hadn't done that since she started the new job.

I was glad Alexis knew something was up, but

I really didn't want to talk about it. And I knew she must be sticking up for me with Katie and Mia, which made me mad to think about, but still thankful.

"I don't think there's anything you can do," I said honestly. "But thank you."

Alexis saluted me. "You're welcome, sarge," she said, trying to lighten things up a little.

"Alexis?" I said. "Can you . . . um . . . can you not mention anything that's going on at home to Katie and Mia?"

Alexis looked like she was going to say something, but she didn't. She nodded yes. "Wouldn't disobey a sergeant!" she said.

And though we both laughed as we went our separate ways, I was left wondering what else the club was discussing without me.

That night, right before dinner, I tapped on Matt and Sam's door. "Matt?"

"Come in," said Matt.

I poked my head in. He was sitting at his desk and Sam was out. "Can you help me with something?" I asked. "I'll pay you," I added before he could say no.

Matt looked at me suspiciously. "Is it something heinous?" he asked.

I came into the room, which was all blue corduroy, sports posters, and team logos. I laid down a piece of paper I had been working on on Matt's desk. "I need to make flyers for my dog-walking business, and I was wondering if you could help me. Because you took that class and all." I held my breath hopefully as Matt studied the information.

He looked up at me.

"Well?" I asked, thinking he was going to make me trade extra Jake days for this.

"Do you really need more responsibilities in your life?" he asked.

I sighed. He kind of sounded like Dad. "I need more money. . . ."

He looked at me for an extra minute, and then he shrugged. "Okay. I'll do it."

"Oh my gosh, you will? Thanks, Matt! I take back every bad thing I ever said about you! Almost."

"No prob," said Matt. "I can probably put something together tonight, okay?"

"Thanks. That would be great. And also"—I laid another piece of paper down on his desk—"will you do some for the Cupcake Club, too?"

Matt took the second sheet of paper. "Sure," he agreed. "Anything that will get me extra cupcakes."

I thanked him again and left the room before he

changed back into the Matt I knew. *Huh,* I thought to myself. *Maybe Matt wasn't all bad.*

By nine that night Matt had two drafts for me to review. He had done a really good job, using cute art and eye-catching fonts. I was psyched, and I could tell Matt was pleased too. I almost wanted to hug him. I offered to watch Jake the next day.

By ten we had printed two stacks of fifty flyers, and then our parents insisted we go to sleep. *That was okay,* I thought, *since fifty new clients would be crazy. For dog walking or cupcakes.*

The next day Jake and I took Jenner on an extra-long walk around the neighborhood and handed out flyers and stuffed them in mailboxes. We stopped at the grocery store and bought a big bag of liver snaps to hand out to any dogs we saw, and Jake proudly wore a T-shirt that I had quickly created for him. It was just like mine, with all the dog-walking info, but his said OFFICER TAYLOR on the back. He loved it.

That night Alexis e-mailed to report they had two new inquiries from the cupcake flyers. "Good work," she said in her sign-off. Katie chimed in with a "Way to go, Emma!" e-mail, which made me feel good.

Phew! I thought, reading the e-mails. Later, four

calls came in for my dog-walking business, and using a chart I made, I scheduled the pickups and drop-offs for all the new dogs for the next day. It would be a lot of work, but I could handle it.

Or maybe I couldn't.

At 4:40 the next afternoon Jake and I were sweating. I had four leashes in my hands, and I could hardly walk down the street as the dogs kept wandering around and twining their leads around one another or around a tree or, worst of all, around my ankles. I'd already had to pick up two poops and leave one behind because it was disgustingly un-pick-up-able. Luckily, the dogs were all family dogs, so they got along pretty well with one another. It hadn't occurred to me that they might fight until we passed a neighbor's house and their dog had run to the property line, barking like mad and baring his teeth at the pack. Two of my dogs strained at their leashes, growling and baring their teeth, and it had taken all my strength to hold on to them. Jake was rattled and teary after the experience, and I was pretty fried. I had to face it: Four dogs was too many to walk at a time. Plus, I still had one more dog to go. Still, at five dollars a walk, I needed all five dogs. I was going to have to figure out a new walking plan.

We reached the corner of Pond Lane, and Jenner stopped to do his business. I sighed and waited patiently, glad for the brief break. Suddenly I heard a bike bell jingling, and I turned around, hoping maybe it was Alexis. It was Sydney and Mags, Sydney's best friend.

"Hey!" called Mags.

I nodded in greeting. I had nothing to say to these girls, and honestly I was so mad that I kept running into them. For some reason they stopped and stood with their bikes between their legs.

"Wow. Are these all yours?" asked Mags incredulously.

"No, I walk them for the neighbors." I was trying to be casual. I didn't need to get into a long chat with Mags right now.

"Good thing," said Sydney. "Your house would stink!" She wrinkled her button nose in distaste.

"I imagine so," I said, in what I hope came off as a "duh." Jenner was done, but I didn't want to bend down and scoop it up while the other girls were there.

"So I think I'm getting the dress from The Special Day," said Sydney casually. It was odd that she mentioned it because she had hardly acknowledged me when they were there on Saturday. Why wasn't she telling Mia this? Wait, did she say "the" dress? As in my dress?

"Oh?" I said fake casually back. "Did they find you another one?"

"No, but there's one still on hold that they ordered and the lady said if it wasn't paid for by next week, then I could have it," said Sydney, shrugging innocently.

My heart lurched. What? That was my dress! And I thought I had two weeks, not one. But if there was only one left . . . So Katie, Alexis, and Mia had already paid for their dresses and mine was still hanging there, alone? When did they go back? And how would I ever make enough money to pay for the dress in one week?

My worry must have shown on my face again because Mags asked, "Are you okay?"

Sydney looked smug. She was so awful.

"No, I'm fine," I said, recovering. "It's just . . ." I looked down at Jenner's work. "I hate this part."

Sydney was still looking at me coolly. "We'll leave you to it," she said. "Tell your friend she only has a week to get her dress!"

I felt sick.

"Or actually . . . What am I saying? Don't tell her!

Then I can have it!" Sydney laughed and pedaled away with Mags.

I stooped to clean up after Jenner, and he licked my hand. I patted him on the head. He really was a good dog. *If only I were a dog,* I thought. *It would be so much easier.*

CHAPTER 9

Mix, Stir . . . Mixed-up

On Friday I more or less sorted out the dog walking. I took the dogs out in pairs and Jenner alone, because he was my original customer and my favorite. It made for a long afternoon, but I was kind of enjoying it, especially since the weather was getting warmer. It wasn't too fun in the rain. But I got to visit all these nice houses and play with friendly dogs.

I really liked the Mellgards' house. They had Marley, a black standard poodle, who wore his fur long and curly rather than cut in any froufrou way. He was a cutie and really sweet. Also Mrs. Mellgard baked as a hobby, and her kitchen had racks of baking sheets and pans in every shape and size, and shiny copper saucepans hung from a rack overhead.

Mrs. Mellgard also had every kind of baking appliance, including a massive cherry red stand mixer. I felt sad every time I saw it. I still dreamed about my pink mixer.

After leaving Marley at the Mellgards', I hustled home. We were baking at Alexis's house tonight, and I absolutely had to be on time. Besides, I was excited to go because we were trying out my new bacon cupcake recipe. I'd have to stop at the Quickie Mart and pick up some ingredients on the way over.

Alexis's house was quiet, so there weren't a lot of distractions. Her sister was at after-school extracurriculars and her parents were at work. The Cupcake Club worked well there. Tonight we were also baking the first official batch of minis for Mona, so I was excited about that, too.

I was determined to try harder. And I did. I was on time, and I took charge with the bacon recipe. I creamed the butter and sugar for the caramel cupcakes in Alexis's mom's mixer. Meanwhile Alexis was making the fondant for Mona's bridal cupcakes, Katie was making the white frosting, and Mia was already filling the mini cupcake tins with little dollops of batter. We weren't as chatty as usual, but I tried to convince myself that it was because we were busy and not because anyone was annoyed with anyone else.

I was wondering what we were going to do over the weekend. We usually did something together. I didn't have any dog-walking jobs over the weekend, unfortunately, because all the owners were home and so didn't need me. So that was two days without income. I was hoping the order from Mona would help make up for some of that loss. I was also dying to talk with the others about Sydney and the dress—in fact, I had been since yesterday—but I couldn't think of any way that didn't mention not being able to pay for it in the first place.

"So what's up for the weekend?" I asked.

I looked up just in time to see Mia and Katie exchange a funny glance, and it gave me a prickly feeling in my chest. What was that all about? I looked at Alexis, whose head was down as she apparently concentrated on the frosting. I wasn't sure if she'd just witnessed something or not. Were Mia and Katie keeping a secret?

"Alexis?" I asked again.

Alexis looked up very innocently, as if she'd been daydreaming before. "Hmm? What?" she asked. She was not a spacey person, so this act did not hold up well.

I was now very suspicious. "What are you doing this weekend?' I asked, enunciating each word distinctly.

"Oh, not much," said Alexis, waving her hand.

This was weird. There was always something going on during the weekends.

"Do you have a soccer game?" I asked as I flipped the bacon out onto a paper towel to drain. I looked back at Alexis again.

"Oh, yeah. Soccer. For sure. And then dinner with my family tomorrow night. Oh, and we'll need a meeting on Sunday. We have to try out a new recipe of Mia's."

Well, this was the first I'd heard of a Sunday meeting, but I would definitely attend. "Hmm. What about you guys this weekend?" I asked the other two again.

They gave similar vague answers—family, chores, homework. They were definitely acting shifty. They all seemed to have a secret, and I wasn't in on it. I wasn't sure whether I should get mad or cry. But then again I had a secret too.

"Hey, let's play a game," suggested Mia in a bright tone of voice, like a nursery school teacher.

"Which one?" I asked, glad for the distraction. "Celebrity Cupcake? Wildest Cupcakes? Name

That Cupcake?" We had lots of cupcake games.

"Name That Cupcake," said Mia. "Definitely."

"You go first," said Alexis as she began molding the fondant into tiny edible flowers.

"Okay. Hmm." Mia thought for a minute. Then she said, "Aha! I've got it! A mocha cake ... with ... butterscotch mini chips throughout and ... fudge frosting ... with ... tiny marshmallows sprinkled across the top! What would you call it? Um, Katie?"

Katie smiled. "Mocha, butterscotch, fudge, and marshmallow? How about 'The Winter Storm'?"

"Lame!" declared Mia. "Alexis?" she prompted.

Alexis tipped her head to the side in a thoughtful pose. Then she said, "Well, if you made it Godiva mocha powder and Ghirardelli chips, with Valrhona fudge frosting, you could call them 'Millionaires' because the ingredients are so fancy!"

"That is so good," I said. "We should do those."

"What's your name suggestion?" Mia asked me.

"Oh. Um." I thought for a second. Alexis's idea was hard to top. "Swampcakes?" I offered, shrugging. "Like really gross-looking, gooey cupcakes that sink in the middle?"

Everyone laughed again.

"I love 'Swampcakes'!" declared Mia. "But actually you could put shredded coconut on top and maybe another kind of mini chip inside to really swamp them. Too bad we can't use nuts. . . ."

The Cupcake Club had a vigilant no-nut policy because so many kids we knew were allergic to nuts. There was simply no point in working with nuts at all.

"I think 'Millionaires' is brilliant, anyway," I said. "Maybe we'll all be cupcake millionaires someday!"

Mia pulled Mona's order of mini cupcakes from the oven. They were perfectly white angel food cake with lightly browned edges. She turned the tin upside down over a cooling rack and tapped it to make all the cupcakes pop out. "Yum," said Mia, reaching for the next tray. "These things are so cute. Such a great size. You could eat ten and not realize it."

"That's the point," said Alexis. "That's why Mona liked them so much. She said brides are so careful about their figures that they're always hungry and therefore often cranky when they come into her store. She liked the minis because they're so irresistible, she figured the brides would eat at least one and it would perk them up."

We all giggled.

"I'm glad my mom's not like that!" said Mia.

"We'll see tomorrow . . . ," started Katie. Then

she stopped abruptly and glanced at me, then Mia.

I was confused. I looked at Mia just in time to see Mia shake her head a tiny, tiny bit at Katie. What was going on? And should I call them on it?

No. Instead I crossed the room and went to crumble the bacon for the bacon cupcake frosting. It might be best to frost the cupcakes and keep the crumbled bacon in a Ziploc bag until it was time to serve the cupcakes; then you could just sprinkle the bacon bits over the tops of the 'cakes and the bacon would still be crispy. I turned to suggest that to the others and discovered them in the midst of a silent conversation made up of wild gestures and gesticulations, as well as mouthed words. It was like they were playing charades.

Everyone froze. Even me, for a second. Then I said, "Guys. What is going on?" I was nervous.

Everyone looked at me. Alexis was the first to speak.

"Emma, um, we feel really funny about this, so we didn't want to tell you. But . . . we bought our dresses for the wedding already, and we're going to go get them fitted tomorrow. We know you haven't bought yours yet, so we didn't say anything."

My face turned hot. I felt humiliated. "Oh," I said. "But if I'd known everyone else had bought theirs . . . I . . . I . . . I would have already bought mine, too!"

Katie and Mia exchanged a look. "Really?" said Mia. She didn't look like she believed me.

"Yeah . . . totally. I just . . . You know, my parents' schedules are pretty off the wall these days, so I just haven't scheduled a time to go down there with one of them."

"Oh . . . ," said Mia skeptically. "Because actually, if you still want to be a junior bridesmaid, um, my mom offered to buy it for you, just so it didn't get sold to someone else. . . ."

I noticed Alexis was looking at me.

"Oh no! I don't need help!" I cried. I must have said it really loudly because Mia flinched. I felt so bad. For me and for Mia. Mostly for me. What was I saying? What was I getting myself into?

"You could pay her back, if you wanted," said Alexis. "So it wouldn't be like she was buying it for you. Just like a loan."

"No. Sorry, thank you, but . . . ," I said. I didn't know what to say. Did they know I couldn't afford it? Alexis may have pieced it together, but I wondered how much she really knew.

"I mean, that is such a nice offer but . . . I mean, no need. And I do still want to be a junior bridesmaid! Of course I do! I . . . I'll go in on . . ." I did a rapid calculation in my head. I figured I'd earn another seventy-five dollars for dog walking by next Wednesday. I might be able to borrow a little from Sam.

I felt like everyone was staring at me. I could do it. I could figure it out for sure. "I'll go in on Wednesday and get it. You can tell Mona."

Mia looked skeptical, but Katie butted in. "Great! Then maybe you should just come to the fitting with us tomorrow!"

"I don't think they will do that until you buy it," said Mia.

I knew Mia was right, but I wished I'd been the one to refuse. It was kind of mean of Mia to say no.

"Yeah," I agreed, shrugging. "I have a lot to do tomorrow anyway, so . . ." That was, of course, not true. But at least I now knew what the other girls were up to tomorrow and why they had been acting so weird and shifty this evening. "So I'll see you on Sunday, and you can tell me all about it."

I thought I was going to cry, so I turned back to the bacon frosting and pretended to be really busy.

Okay! Be organized! Be efficient! I told myself. *I'll figure it out.*

I dipped a finger in the frosting, then tasted it.

It was insanely good. I sighed heavily. At least one thing was going right. Bacon cupcakes. *Oh, and also the dog walking,* I thought. The dog walking was good. Bacon and dogs. Well, at least they go together.

CHAPTER 10

On Thin Icing

The next morning the phone rang and it was Mrs. Mellgard. She had a change of plans and wondered if I was free to take Marley out for a long walk and playdate. She'd be willing to pay me double. Ten dollars! I jumped at the chance and said I'd be right over.

On my way out the door I loaded my pocket with liver snaps for Marley, then grabbed two of the remaining four bacon cupcakes from the night before for Mrs. Mellgard. The cupcakes were, if I do say so myself, delicious. The ribbons of salty caramel burst in your mouth when you took a bite of the sweet yellow cake, and the bacon gave a satisfying crunch as the frosting swirled across the roof of your mouth. Everyone had adored them; Sam had had four when he got home from work. One for each movie pass, he joked.

At the Mellgards', I left the cupcakes on the counter with a note for Mrs. Mellgard, then took Marley out for a good time. It was a nice day, and I tried not to think about everyone trying on the dress. The fresh air felt good and so did running around with Marley. When I got back after more than two hours of Frisbee and running with Marley, Mrs. Mellgard was back and standing in the kitchen.

"Emma!" she cried. "Oh my God!"

I was alarmed. "What?" I cried. Had I been gone too long? Was Mrs. Mellgard worried about Marley? I really should have checked my watch.

Mrs. Mellgard grasped at her chest. "The bacon cupcakes. Oh my God!"

"What?" I was panicked now. Had I accidentally baked something into a cupcake? For a second I thought maybe I poisoned Mrs. Mellgard. Then I saw her smile.

"They are the *best* thing I have ever tasted! Wow! Thank you so much!"

I grinned, relieved. "I'm glad you liked them. I really like them too."

"Like them? I love them!" said Mrs. Mellgard

giddily. "I wonder . . . is there any chance you might have time to make me some for my book club meeting on Wednesday?"

"Sure!" I said, without even really thinking about it. "I'd love to. How many do you need?"

"About two dozen, considering my husband will probably have four." Mrs. Mellgard laughed.

"Done. I'll deliver them on Wednesday around six, okay?"

"Great. What do I owe you?" asked Mrs. Mellgard.

"Oh, we usually charge thirty dollars for two dozen." I wasn't supposed to do this. I was supposed to run all orders by the club so we could agree and prioritize and price them. But . . . well . . . I needed the thirty dollars. I knew it was wrong. But Operation Dream Dress was about to be a bust. I had to do something.

"Who's we?" asked Mrs. Mellgard with interest.

"Well, three of my friends are in a Cupcake Club with me. We bake for parties and events. We're actually baking cupcakes for a wedding!"

"Well!" said Mrs. Mellgard. "Sign me up!"

It wasn't until I skipped down the driveway that I realized I should be heading back to Mona at The Special Day on Wednesday to purchase the dress.

I felt nervous again. Well, I'd just have to make it work.

On Sunday I had another dog emergency. The Jensens' daughter's swim team had made it into the finals at a tournament out of state, and their labradoodle, Wendy, needed walking while they were gone, in the morning and afternoon. Since it was a weekend I had the whole day to fit the walks in, so it was okay. I just had to do it before the Cupcake Club meeting. But part of me wanted to miss the Cupcake Club meeting. I was tired of Mia's looks and people talking behind my back. And in all honesty, I wasn't sure I could bear sitting through a reenactment of the magical hours spent at The Special Day. So like a coward, instead of calling, I sent off an e-mail to the group saying something had come up and I couldn't make the meeting. I knew it was lame. But when I pressed send, part of me was proud for doing it. After all, I didn't need those girls if they were going to be so mean. And I could do my own cupcake orders. I already did, with Mrs. Mellgard.

Katie and Mia didn't reply. Alexis e-mailed right back with "Are you okay?" *No,* I thought miserably. I hit delete without responding.

On Monday at school Mia and Katie were okay

but distant. Nobody asked what my emergency was yesterday, and I didn't ask how Mia's special recipe turned out. Alexis kept trying to talk to me, but I brushed her off. At lunch I managed to squeeze in a flute session in one of the music department's practice rooms, so I avoided the lunch table. I told myself I was just being organized and making the most of my time. But I knew I just didn't want to deal.

On Monday night I thought about telling Mom about the dress. But Mom seemed to have forgotten about it and, anyway, I just didn't know how to bring it up. As the days went on, Mom looked more and more tired, and she and Dad seemed worried.

I went to my room and laid all my money out to count, including today's dog-walking receipts. I calculated the thirty dollars I'd get from Mrs. Mellgard on Wednesday. The cupcake expenses were probably around fifteen dollars, so that was really only fifteen dollars profit. *Wow,* I thought coldly, *I can make a lot more money if I don't have to split it four ways.* Then I thought of my friends. I missed them.

Later that night there was an e-mail from Alexis requesting an emergency meeting of the Cupcake Club on Wednesday to discuss three impending new orders that needed to be addressed. Wednesday. Alexis didn't do her usual "Hi, Cupcakers" or sign off with "XOXO." Something was up. Plus, it was on Wednesday. Right in the middle of baking, walking the dogs, and buying the dress (if that could even happen). How was I going to do it all? And what's more, was it really to discuss new orders or were they calling the meeting to vote me out? I stared at the e-mail, trying to read between the lines. Alexis had sent another e-mail: "Call me." Nobody else replied.

Just then there was a knock on the door.

"Who is it?" I demanded crankily, hustling to gather up the money.

"It's me," said Matt.

"Come in," I barked. Great, now I probably had to watch Jake on top of everything else. I began folding the money to put back into the cosmetic bag I kept it in.

Matt opened the door. "Wow. That's a lot of money," he said first. Then, when I didn't comment, he shrugged. "Hey, is the favor department open?" he asked.

I sighed. After Matt had been so nice about the flyers, I felt I had to say yes. "Sure. What do you need?" I asked.

"Uh, do you think you could bake some bacon cupcakes for my team dinner? It's Wednesday."

Of course it is, I thought. "But Wednesday is a Jake day for you," I said with my voice shaking.

"Well, that's the other thing. I can do Jake from pickup till five thirty if you can take over after that. Then I'll owe you two hours."

Wednesday was starting to look like it would be the worst day of my life: I had to bake cupcakes for Mrs. Mellgard, walk three dogs, babysit Jake, make it to a Cupcake Club meeting to get kicked out, and somehow find time to buy the bridesmaid dress before Sydney. How was this all going to happen? But I did owe Matt. *I can do it,* I tried to cheer myself on. *If I just say it, it always gets done.*

"I'll pay you . . . ," Matt offered, eyeing my pile of money again.

"No, you don't need to pay me," I said. "I'll do it. And I'll take Jake." I should be all done by six thirty anyway. It would be okay as long as I was organized.

Matt smiled a huge smile. "That's awesome. People are going to freak out over those cupcakes. Thanks."

"Sure," I said, returning the smile. That was as much of a compliment as I would ever get from Matt.

"So what's all that money for, anyway?" asked Matt.

I shrugged. "Well, it's not enough for anything, right now. I need to buy a two-hundred-and-fifty-dollar bridesmaid's dress on Wednesday, or my enemy will get it and my so-called friends will officially also become my enemies. And I don't want to ask Mom and Dad to help me. I'll probably get kicked out of the wedding party and kicked out of the Cupcake Club. So actually, I don't know what this money is for." I zipped the cosmetic bag closed.

"Wow. It's expensive being a girl," said Matt, half teasing.

"It sure is," I said angrily.

Matt hesitated, as if he was going to say something but then didn't. He left, closing the door gently behind him and leaving me feeling sadder and lonelier than I had all day.

But on Tuesday I was feeling in control. It was a Jake day, but I only had two dogs to walk. I decided I'd get the dogs, then meet Jake's bus, then take them all to Quickie Mart to pick up the baking supplies for the bacon cupcake bakeathon the next day. It should be no problem. I had a plan. I felt good.

But what I hadn't banked on was Franco the

dachshund having diarrhea. Yes, it was a total mess and a total bummer. He must've eaten something in his house that made him sick because when I showed up, he had pooped all over the kitchen. Though it technically was not my job to clean it up, I didn't feel right leaving it. So I went around with cleaning spray and paper towels, then pocketed a wad of emergency paper towels and headed out to get the other dog. But now I was behind schedule. I knew I should just go home and wait for Jake's bus, but I also didn't want to just sit and wait, and I was better off having both dogs ready to go when Jake got home so we could then head in the other direction to the Quickie Mart.

Unfortunately, I didn't realize how long it would take me to get home. Again. By the time I got home, the bus had passed our house. I could see it a block up ahead. I set out chasing it, but Franco was butt-scooching across the pavement and couldn't be rushed. I tied the dogs to a pole and set out at a dead sprint to get to the bus, nearly getting hit by a car in the process. I had to catch it. They wouldn't let Jake off unless there was someone there. I ran faster than I ever ran before and caught up to the bus on the next stop as the door was closing, and waved at Sal the driver. Sal opened the door and called to Jake, but he had a concerned look on his face.

"Hey, Emma, I'm sorry, but I have to write you up for missing the bus today," Sal said. "I hate to do it, but it puts my job in jeopardy if I don't follow the protocol." He shrugged. "Sorry."

I sighed heavily in defeat. I understood. I had messed up and Sal was just doing his job, but the timing was terrible. If you got more than one write-up, you couldn't take the bus anymore. Dad was going to freak out. "Okay," I said, then nodded and tried to look as bad as I felt, hoping Sal would take pity on me. "I'm really sorry."

Jake came wearily down the stairs. He had fallen asleep on the bus again; I could tell by the way his hair was sticking up. "You forgot me!" he yelled.

"No, I didn't, Jakey." I sighed. "I was just late."

Here we go again, I thought. There would be no trip to the Quickie Mart. Not with Jake in one of his moods. We trudged down the block to the waiting dogs. I decided I'd be better off just taking them to our yard. That way I could get Jake home.

I sent Jake in to watch TV, and then I played with the dogs for half an hour. Franco had diarrhea two more times, and I had to get out the hose to spray it away, but the yard still smelled like dog poop. Eventually I had to get Jake to come with me to take the dogs home. Jake complained the whole way, but I managed to drop them off without Franco having another mess. "Let's go to the Quickie Mart now," I said cheerily. "I need a few things."

"I don't wanna," said Jake. I hoped he would just keep walking anyway. But as we passed our house on the way, Dad was standing in the doorway, his mouth set in a grim line and his hands on his hips.

"Hey, Dad's home!" Jake cried, running up the driveway.

"Jake, run up to your room to play for a minute. Emma and I need to have a little discussion," said Dad in his most steely, no-nonsense soccer-coach voice. I felt scared. This would not be good.

"Let's go sit in the kitchen," said Dad. He spoke firmly and decisively, but he did not seem angry as much as disappointed. That was worse.

"Emma, Sal told me you actually missed the bus once before," he said. "This is the third strike. You know what that means."

I wiggled nervously in my seat. I had learned never to offer up a punishment, but rather to wait until it was doled out. In the past I had made the mistake of suggesting something that turned out to be worse than what was coming.

"No more dogs. No more cupcakes. Just school, flute, and Jake."

"But . . . ," I began. What on Earth was I going to do about tomorrow? The most-booked day ever?

"No buts. You were fairly warned. Tomorrow you will come straight home from school and get right to work. That's all."

"But I have commitments," I protested.

"Call them and explain that you are no longer free. It won't be the end of the world," said Dad. "You haven't been employed by any of these people for very long. Though I'm sure they adore you, and rightly so, they did manage to get along just a week or two ago, before you started with them."

"But the cupcakes . . ."

Dad nodded. "We will revisit that issue next week. I think a week off is a very wise idea. Your friends will understand," he said.

"No they won't!" I wailed. "And the dress!" I cried, but instantly regretted it.

"What dress?" asked Dad, a look of confusion on his face.

Just then Matt walked in. He took quick stock of

the scene and put his hands in the air in a gesture of surrender. "Just passing through," he said, and he dashed up the stairs.

Dad looked at me. "What dress?"

"Oh, never mind!" I sobbed, and stood up from the table to leave.

"Do we understand each other?" asked Dad.

I nodded miserably.

"Okay, then," he said.

No, it was not. It was not okay at all.

CHAPTER 11

Add One Sweet Brother

There was a knock on my door later. It was Mom, home from work. I had eaten the hamburger Dad made for dinner in stony silence, finished my homework (the best job I'd done in weeks, even I had to admit), and I was practicing my flute. I was trying hard to not think about cupcakes or dogs or dresses.

"Come in," I said, pausing with the flute at my chin.

Mom opened the door. "It sounded lovely from outside," she said.

I rolled my eyes. "I was only doing scales." I was cranky and even a little mad at Mom, even though I knew none of this was really her fault. I got myself into this mess.

"Honey, we need to talk," said Mom.

First Dad, now Mom. I sighed and put down the flute.

"I heard about what happened with the school bus. Again, I am so sorry that I have put this on you, with my new work schedule and all. I don't think it will be for too much longer, though. It's looking like they might be able to end my work suspension soon. A foundation has kicked in some money for staffing the library so that could be great news for us." Mom smiled brightly.

"Great," I said softly. It was great. It was just probably a little too late.

"Dad told me you had a lot on your plate. I was wondering if there's anything I can help you with?" Mom asked.

Well, I thought, *how about: a trip to the Quickie Mart, baking four dozen bacon cupcakes going to two locations, calling the dog-walking clients to let them know I had to cancel, attending an emergency Cupcake Club meeting, taking care of Jake, and oh, yes, buying the dress.* I really thought I could handle everything. And tonight was the first time I realized maybe I couldn't.

"Honey?" prodded Mom.

"No, thanks," I said finally. I couldn't handle it,

121

but that didn't mean Mom had to.

Mom looked like she didn't believe me. She paused for a minute, watching me carefully. Then she said, "Well, how are the wedding plans coming along? Did they settle on a dress?"

I knew I should tell her. This was the perfect opportunity. And I don't know why I didn't. "Almost, I think," I said. "Pretty close."

Mom smiled. "Well, at least that's something to look forward to. When's the wedding? A month from now?"

"Three weeks," I said. Three very short weeks in which to buy a dress and have it altered. Three very long weeks in which your best friends are not talking to you.

"Wow, they'd better get going on those dresses," said Mom. She put her hands on her knees. "Well, I have to go to the grocery store really quickly to pick up some milk. Is there anything I can get for you?" She stood up.

Well . . .

"Honey?"

Okay, I thought. *I need help.* Mom has always said she would always help me and all I had to do was ask. I thought about it for a while. Then I said, "Yes. I promised Matt I'd make cupcakes for his team dinner tomorrow." I didn't tell her about Mrs. Mellgard. I was still trying to figure out if I could make four dozen cupcakes and deliver them without anyone noticing.

I got a piece of paper and wrote a list of ingredients for the bacon cupcakes.

"No problem," said Mom. "And I think it's very nice that you're doing this for Matt. I'm so happy to see the family pulling together." Then she gave me a kiss. I felt guilty. We might be pulling together, but I was falling apart inside.

Late that night I went online and e-mailed my dog-walking clients to say that due to an unforeseen workload, I would have to put them on a waiting list for the time being. I didn't want to admit I'd been grounded. In my e-mail to Mrs. Mellgard, I made it clear that the cupcakes would still be delivered on time tomorrow (how, I was not sure), and I let Mrs. Anderson know that Jenner would be the first dog off the waiting list when my normal workload resumed.

Next I e-mailed the Cupcake Club to say that I was so sorry, but I would have to miss the meeting the next day. I kept it brief. I was fully prepared to be kicked out. And I knew I wouldn't be a bridesmaid.

Alexis wrote back right away: "Please tell me what's going on."

But I couldn't. I didn't think she would understand and, besides, I didn't want to. My real friends should want to be my friends even if I couldn't be a bridesmaid. I shouldn't have to prove that I was pulling my weight. I was pulling plenty.

Still, I couldn't sleep that night, and I checked my e-mail again first thing the next morning, but there still wasn't any response from Katie or Mia. I was nervous to get to lunch, and I wondered if they would even let me sit with them. Or if I wanted to.

But when I got to the cafeteria, it was Sydney I ran into first.

"Hey! I'm going to get the dress today!" said Sydney, all dressed up in a tight, sleeveless turtleneck and a miniskirt. "I guess your friend never coughed up the dough."

"How do you know . . . I mean, how did you hear?" I asked, my face getting hot.

"I called the store to check, silly!" said Sydney brightly. "I'm going tonight with my mom and Brandi, right after cheerleading. I can't wait!" She flounced away, leaving me standing alone, breathless in the middle of the cafeteria.

I saw Mia, Alexis, and Katie staring at me, already

eating. They hadn't waited for me in our usual meeting spot, which wasn't a total surprise, but it was a pretty strong move on their part. I took a long look at them, gulped, then turned and fled. "Emma!" I heard Alexis calling. But I didn't turn around. I just kept going. I'd eat my lunch alone, in the gym, with all the weirdos. *I'd better get used to it,* I thought bitterly.

I managed to avoid everyone all day, even Alexis, who almost tried to chase me down the hall. After school I ran out the door to the bike rack and pedaled home furiously. I had decided to ask Sam to drop off the cupcakes for Mrs. Mellgard on his way to work. I thought I could hear Alexis calling me again, but I didn't turn around. I hated everyone right now. If they couldn't understand, then I didn't want to be friends with them anyway.

At home I went into a baking frenzy, relieved that Mom had bought the baking supplies the previous night. Matt had met Jake at the bus and taken him to the park for a while to get him out of my hair while I got the cupcakes ready, and I was grateful for that. Jake was the last thing I could handle right now. The cupcakes were cooling on a rack and the frosting and bacon was sitting mixed and crumbled and ready, when the phone rang.

I went to answer it and saw that it was The Special Day bridal salon! What should I say? I couldn't let it go to voice mail because then Mom or Dad would get the message. I picked up the phone, cold with fear and dread.

"Hello?"

"Hello, is Emma there please? This is Patricia from The Special Day bridal salon."

"This is Emma," I said, gulping.

"Oh, hello, dear. I was just calling to see if you could come into the store today. We had set aside the dress for you for Ms. Vélaz's wedding, and Mona is getting nervous about the alterations as the time draws near."

I realized that Patricia was being nice. Instead of saying that I couldn't pay for it, Patricia merely suggested that I was late.

"Oh," I said. "I'm . . . I'm not sure I can make it today."

There was a pause. "Well . . . I can ask Mona about extending the hold period for another day or so. I just have another customer who is eager for the dress. You are going to go ahead with it, are you not?"

"Uh . . ." I had to think.

"Let's do this," said Patricia. "If you can get in

here today, I can legitimately hold off the other customer for another couple of days, or I can put her in a different dress. I think once you see the dress again, you'll realize how marvelous it is on you and you'll be able to organize everything very quickly. Okay?"

I didn't know what to say. I should have said, "Oh, let Sydney have the dress. End my friendship with Mia, Katie, and Alexis. I'm going to quit the Cupcake Club." It was all done already anyway, pretty much. But what I said was, "Okay."

"Great. Then we'll see you soon," said Patricia. "Bye!"

I hung up. I went to frost the cupcakes and put them in their carriers. I was halfway through packing them up when Sam came in, banging the back door.

"Oh! Please tell me those are bacon cupcakes!" he cried happily.

I smiled, despite my gloom. I had made a few extra, partially in hopes of buttering up Sam.

"Yes, Sammy, these are for you." I handed him the plate. "And now I have a favor to ask."

"Uh-oh," he said, through a mouthful of cupcake.

"I need you to drop these off for me in half an

hour. Two dozen go to the Mellgards' on Race Lane. And two dozen go to the gym with Matt, for his team party."

"Ugh," said Sam with a sigh. He thought for a second. "I guess I can do it," he said. And he grabbed another cupcake.

Just then his cell phone rang. "Hello?" he said.

I was so happy I could kiss him. I packed up the rest of Matt's cupcakes. All set.

"Where? What? Dude, slow down," said Sam in annoyance.

I glanced at him and saw that he was looking at me, his eyebrows knit together in concern.

What? I mouthed at him, but he didn't react. What did I do now?

"Okay, let me just write down the address. Darn it all, I'm going to be late for work tonight," he huffed. "Bye."

"What was that all about?" I asked, a little worried. "Is everything all right?" I pressed the tops down on the carriers. Sam was looking at me strangely.

"Nothing," he said finally. "I'll be ready in twenty. But you're coming with me," he said. "You can run in with the cupcakes while I wait in the car. It'll be faster." And he left the kitchen in a hurry.

"What? But I have Jake! And Dad will kill me if we leave!" I called after him. "Sam!" but he didn't come back.

Ten minutes later, Jake and Matt walked in, and Matt ran to shower and change. He gave me a strange look, one that made me say, "What?" in annoyance, but he didn't answer.

Jake actually helped wash the baking dishes—sort of—and shortly after we finished, Sam came down, freshly showered, followed by Matt, also freshly showered, with a backpack. Something about Sam still looked fishy, but I wasn't going to press it, especially since I needed his help.

"Let's hit it, kids," Sam said, grabbing the keys to the minivan.

"What about Mom and Dad?" I asked. I couldn't deal with more punishment.

"I'll deal with them later," said Sam.

The novelty of going anywhere with Sam was enough to make Jake cooperate, even without a bribe. But he was curious. "Where are we going, Sammy?" asked Jake.

"Down to the station house," said Sam with a wink. "We're going to book her." And he jerked his thumb at me. I rolled my eyes and decided to go along with it all. If Sam was willing to deal with

Mom and Dad, then how much trouble could I get into? The four of us got into the minivan and set off to drop off the Mellgards' cupcakes, Matt and his cupcakes, and return home. Or so I thought.

CHAPTER 12

Brothers and Bridesmaids

$\mathcal{E}$xcept that we didn't go straight home. After the cupcake delivery to the Mellgards', which went smoothly, and dropping off Matt, Sam turned his car in the opposite direction of home.

"Hey! Where are you going?" I asked in alarm. I was already treading on thin ice. I knew my parents would kill me for dragging Jake around this late and not doing my homework. Plus, no one had started dinner.

"Just downtown for a minute. Chill."

Now I was annoyed. This week was just getting worse by the day. I turned and glared out the window. Then I turned back to Sam.

"Are we going to the mall?" I asked. Maybe I could run into The Special Day after all and tie up the loose ends. Just tell Patricia thanks anyway, but it wasn't going to happen. I didn't want her to be mad at me. I looked over at Jake in the backseat, and I suddenly spied Matt's backpack.

"Sam! We have to go back! Matt left his bag!" I said urgently. I didn't want to open it because it was probably stinky, but I was pretty sure his practice clothes were in there.

"Oh," Sam waved his hand. "I'll . . . I'll deal with that," he said.

"But . . ." Then I sighed. Everyone was weird and getting weirder. The cupcakes were delivered. The dress was gone. I was done.

We parked in the mall lot and headed in. Sam carried Matt's backpack. "What are you doing with that?" I asked, but Sam kept walking fast and didn't answer. Sam was walking briskly right toward The Special Day. *What on Earth was going on,* I wondered. Poor Jake was jogging alongside to keep up with Sam's long strides.

"Sam! Slow down! What's the rush?" I asked breathlessly. "And where are we going?"

"I can't be too late for work," said Sam. "There's a six-thirty show, and they need me."

And then we were there: The Special Day.

Sam held the door and ushered us in.

"I . . . I . . ." I didn't know what to say. Did Sam know? Was he going to make me apologize to Patricia and Mona for telling them I was going to buy the dress?

Sam strode to the counter, and all I could do was follow him.

"May I help you?" asked Patricia, gliding to the counter. "Oh, hello there! You came in after all!" said Patricia to me.

I blushed furiously. Now I was going to have to explain it all in front of my brothers.

"Hey! It was you!" said an indignant voice behind me. I whirled around to find Sydney Whitman standing there with her mother and cousin, the tarty Brandi.

"Wh-wh-at?" I said.

"You were the one who hadn't bought the dress! But then why are you here now? I came to get it!" Sydney's eyes flashed angrily.

I felt mad all of a sudden. That was my dress. And Sydney was not going to take it from me. Sam and Patricia were in an intense conversation, their heads nearly touching. Then Patricia waved Sam to the back of the store to Mona's office.

I just stood there, not knowing what to do.

"I guess they're going to get the dress for me

after all," said Sydney smugly. "So who's that hot-tie?" she asked, flipping her hair.

"My brother," I said. "And he has a girlfriend." Sam did not have a girlfriend. Not one I knew about, at least. But it sure wasn't going to be Sydney.

Before Sydney could say anything else, I saw Alexis, Katie, and Mia walking from the back of the store. With Mona, Sam, and Patricia!

"What is going on?" I almost cried. I was so confused.

Mona had the dress on a hanger, and she crossed behind the counter, hung it on a pole, and waved me over to her.

I was so embarrassed. Now everyone was going to hear me turn down the dress, and they'd all witness Sydney's glory as she purchased it. I felt like I was walking off a cliff as I walked over to Mona.

"Honey," whispered Mona. "You have a lot of people who love you. You must be a very special person."

I didn't even hear her. I just started to cry. "I'm sorry, but . . . I can't buy the dress." I started crying really hard then, and I couldn't stop.

"Oh no, sweetheart. Please, don't cry. Everything is all right." She gestured at Patricia for a Kleenex, and Patricia scurried to grab one from one of the many nearby boxes.

"I have your dress all ready for you," Mona continued, as if she hadn't heard me at all. "We'll just have you try it on and then we can fit it."

"But you don't understand. . . . I can't afford it," I said. "I'm sorry I let it go on so long. I didn't know how to tell you. Any of you," I said, turning to look at the Cupcakers.

"Oh, Emma!" cried Mia, and she ran over and hugged me. Alexis and Katie piled on.

"I know you all hate me. I'm so sorry," I said. "I couldn't go to the meetings because I was trying to make extra money dog walking. And I had to babysit. And . . . and . . . well, I guess I just couldn't do it all." I didn't even mention the order for Mrs. Mellgard.

"We don't hate you!" said Mia.

"Why didn't you tell us?" said Katie. "We could have helped you."

"They did help you!" interjected Mona. "These girls came down here today to negotiate a reduced rate for your dress. And we've struck a deal!"

Alexis smiled. "Mona is knocking ninety-nine dollars off of the dress in exchange for four weeks of mini cupcakes!" said Alexis.

"This one drives a hard bargain," said Mona, gesturing at Alexis. "She's coming to work for me one day."

Alexis beamed.

"But how did you know I was . . . that I couldn't afford it?" I asked.

"I e-mailed your brother last night," said Alexis. "When I didn't hear back from you, I knew something was really wrong, and well, I knew about your mom's job. I asked Matt if he knew about the dress, and he put two and two together."

I remembered Sam was there, and I turned around to look at him. He smiled and shrugged.

"Matt e-mailed me and told me that he and Sam wanted to chip in for the dress for you, but we still didn't have enough," said Alexis. "So I decided to see if we could work out a deal for you. And, well, I told Katie and Mia. Please don't be mad. I just wanted them to know the real reason you hadn't been around."

"You should have told us!" said Mia. "I just thought you didn't care about the wedding and didn't want to be in the club! We could have helped you figure it out. Or I wouldn't have cared if you wore an old dress!"

"I don't know what to say," I said. I really didn't.

So many people helped me: Alexis, Mia, Katie, Sam, even Matt.

"Well, instead of saying anything, let's go get that dress on," said Mona. "We need to make sure it fits you perfectly."

"Wait! That's my dress!" shrieked Sydney.

We turned to look—we had completely forgotten about her.

"Now, dear, we have a lot to discuss," said Mona smoothly, and she steered Sydney away from us as she cast a strong look at Patricia to manage the rest of the situation.

I was on cloud nine as I stumbled into the dressing room, and once the dress was on, I felt even better. I still couldn't believe my brothers had done this. I mean, Matt? And my friends. It was amazing. I thought for a second about how much heartache I would have saved myself if I had just told them from the start. Live and learn, as Dad always says.

I smiled in the mirror. The dress really was gorgeous.

There was a knock on the door.

"Come in," I said.

Jake stuck his head around the corner. "Wow, Emmy! You look like a princess fairy!" he said breathlessly.

I laughed. "Thanks, Jakey."

The door opened wider. And there was Mom. "Oh, honey," she said, and she burst into tears. "I saw Sam when I was leaving work, and I was so confused. . . . You look beautiful!"

I laughed as Alexis handed Mom a Kleenex from one of three nearby boxes.

"Doesn't she look divine?" asked Alexis, and all of us started giggling.

CHAPTER 13

Sweet Endings

That night all of us (minus Jake, who was asleep in his bed) sat in the kitchen, a plate of bacon cupcakes on the table. It was late and everyone was tired but very, very happy.

Mom was happy because the director of the library had called to say that the new grant funding would cover reinstating her job, and that she'd be back on board as of the first of the month, which was in only eight days.

Matt was happy because the bacon cupcakes had been a huge hit at his team dinner; his coach had even implied that someone with the great idea of bringing such delicious cupcakes to a team dinner ought to be captain next year. Matt was thrilled.

Sam was happy because he could have his Friday

nights back once Mom went back to work at the library. He had been missing out on the best shift at the movie theater and hanging out with his friends afterward.

Dad was happy because Mom was going back to work and because his kids were happy.

And I was happiest of all. I had amazing friends, generous brothers, a dad who had revoked my punishment once he heard the reasons why I was so overworked, and a mom who was going back to a normal work schedule. I also had a gorgeous dress that was being altered to fit me and permission to run the dog-walking business one weekday and one weekend day each week for two hours. Plus, Mrs. Mellgard had just called to place a very large order and was referring the Cupcake Club to all her friends. I had come clean about that order earlier. No one was angry, and Alexis was really happy we had another client.

"This has been a crazy few weeks," said Mom.

"Tell me about it," I said.

"Honey, I'm so sorry that Dad and I were so out of touch with what was going on in your life. I just feel awful about it," Mom said.

"That's okay," I said. "After all, I can always handle . . ." And I trailed off.

140

Dad looked at me.

"Emma, you know we're always here for you. Please don't let things get that out of control again without asking one of us for help or at least filling us in on what's going on, okay? You're lucky you have such great brothers, kiddo." He nodded toward Matt and Sam.

"The greatest," I said.

"Just don't stop baking, even if all else fails," said Matt, laughing as he peeled the wrapper from a cupcake he'd just snagged.

"Yes, cupcakes should be the last thing to go, after schoolwork and flute," agreed Sam through a mouthful of cupcake.

"I just can't wait until the wedding," I said dreamily.

"Speaking of weddings, who was that cute girl in the bridal salon? The blonde?" asked Sam.

"Aaargh!" I groaned. Maybe Sam wasn't the greatest brother ever!

On the day of Mia's mom's wedding the Cupcake Club, minus Mia, was meeting at my house to put the final touches on the bridal cupcakes and the groom's cake, which was the bacon cupcakes, of course. I now thought of them as my lucky recipe.

Mia's mom had decided to go with the sheet of minis in the shape of a heart for her wedding dessert. She had sampled some at Mona's during her final fitting and found them irresistible. The club decided to do them just like Mona's: angel food cake, white fondant frosting, and white sugar flowers as decoration. There would be a heart made of raspberry cupcakes with pink frosting in the center of the sheet of cupcakes on the buffet.

At eight thirty that Saturday morning, I heard a quiet knock on the back door. It was Alexis. She had already been to The Special Day and dropped off Mona's cupcakes that we'd made the night before. Now she was ready to work some more.

"Hi," she whispered.

"Hi," I whispered back. "We don't have to whisper. There's no one here."

"Where is everyone?" whispered Alexis.

"Practice," I said in a normal voice. We both laughed.

There was another knock on the door. It was Katie.

"Hey," she whispered.

"No whispering," whispered Alexis. We started laughing really hard. Katie gave us a look that said she thought we were cuckoo, and she came in.

142

We each ate a big bowl of cereal and then got down to business. I was making the bacon, and Katie was making the fondant frosting for the white minis; she would set aside a bit of my buttercream frosting and tint it pink with raspberry jam for the pink cupcakes. Alexis was working on the edible sugar flower decorations, which were kind of hard, but Alexis did them perfectly, of course.

"Anyone talked to Mia yet?" I asked.

"I e-mailed her this morning to say good luck," said Katie.

"I think they were going to a spa this morning with her aunts and cousins," said Alexis. "Group rate, I bet. Probably a wedding package."

I rolled my eyes at Katie, and we both giggled. *Oh, Alexis.*

The bacon was done, nice and crispy. I set it on paper towels to dry and turned to make the buttercream. We were tripling the recipe, which meant three boxes of confectioners' sugar, six sticks of softened butter, three teaspoons of vanilla, and almost a half a cup of milk. The hand mixer groaned and strained against the ingredients and gave off a light smell of burning plastic. This was nothing new, but it was all part of the reason I still wanted that new pink mixer.

It felt so good to be with my friends again. But I guess we were talking so much that we kind of lost track of time.

"Oh no!" cried Alexis as she looked at the clock. "How will we get this done?"

I started to panic. "I can . . . I will . . ." Then I stopped.

Mom, Jake, Sam, Dad, and Matt came in.

I took a deep breath. "Mom!" I cried. "Mom, we need help!"

Mom smiled. "Okay, whatever it is, we can handle it. Come on, guys," she said, gesturing to the boys. "Everybody's in on this one."

"We can do this!" said Alexis, and she smiled at me. "Emma and I can figure out a plan."

And we did. Mom whipped up the buttercream, Dad began packing frosted minis, Jake crumbled the bacon ("Yes, you can taste it. But only once, or I'll arrest you!" I said), Matt helped Katie frost the bacon cupcakes as soon as they were ready, and Sam started carrying boxes out to Dad's station wagon. Alexis and Katie rushed to help him.

With everyone else running around I suddenly realized I didn't have much to do. The kitchen was a hive of busy activity, and everyone was doing his or her job well. I went to check my e-mail. Mia had sent all the club members an e-mail asking us to be at her house a shade earlier. I also had an e-mail from Williams-Sonoma, announcing a new version of the stand mixer. It cost $199! A price reduction! I smiled. The day just kept getting better and better. *Someday,* I thought, *you really will be mine!*

CHAPTER 14

The Special Day

I couldn't wait to put on the dress. Mom buttoned me up and helped brush out my hair. She got a little teary again. Then I went downstairs, where Dad, Sam, Matt, and Jake were all waiting.

"Wow!" said Dad.

"You look so pretty," said Jake.

I blushed a little bit. I wasn't used to everyone looking at me.

"You do look good," said Sam.

Matt nodded.

Dad snapped a few pictures, then we picked up Alexis and Katie and got to Mia's house right on time. Mia opened the door in her matching dress.

Behind her, Ms. Vélaz came floating down the

stairs, and we all just stared at her. I'd never seen anyone look more beautiful.

"Come on, my beautiful bridesmaids," she said. "We're off to get married!" We all giggled and followed her outside to the limousine, which would take us to the ceremony. We had never been in one before, and we were all excited.

I tried to take in everything, but it all went so fast. First we posed for pictures, and then we lined up to go down the aisle. I was a little nervous, but I did it slowly like Mom had practiced with me and I smiled, just like Mia's mom told us. We stood under the canopy and I was looking around and then—bam—it was over and we had to walk back up the aisle.

The party got underway, and we all sat together at a table with lots of pink roses. We were having such a good time. I had never been to a fancy party like this before. Then the band started playing, and we all jumped up to dance.

The cupcakes were a big hit. Everyone loved them, and everyone really chowed down on the bacon cupcakes. "Oh," a woman said, stuffing a few in her purse, "these are divine."

"Did she say 'divine'?" Alexis shrieked, and we all burst into giggles.

"What can I say," said Alexis. "You were right about the bacon!"

"Hey, in a house with three brothers, I know bacon!" I said.

"Emma," said Mia. "You have to promise us something."

I looked up, a little worried by her tone. Katie and Alexis were looking at me too.

"You have to promise us that whatever it is, good or bad, you won't keep secrets from us. Friends tell one another everything, and they help out. I want you to promise that you won't be embarrassed about anything and feel like you can't talk to us."

"I know," I said, hanging my head. I still couldn't believe all that they did for me. I looked down at my beautiful dress. "I'm really sorry. I won't keep anything from you again."

"Honey, this is for you." Mia's mom was at my side. She handed me a white envelope. "It's just a little something I'm giving to each of you as a traditional bridesmaid gift. Thank you for helping to make this such a special day."

"Oh, Ms. Vélaz . . . I mean Mrs. Valdes!"

"I know!" said Mia's mom, rolling her eyes. "I went from Vélaz to Valdes! It's going to confuse everyone."

"I don't know what to say!" I blushed. I hadn't expected a gift.

Mia's mom planted a kiss on top of my head. "Don't say a word," she said. "Just get yourself something you've really wanted." Then she winked at me. She handed a box to Alexis and one to Katie before gliding off.

I looked down at the envelope. I put it on my lap, not wanting to appear greedy, but I was really curious.

"Open them!" said Mia.

Alexis opened a beautiful set of stationery, a journal, and notepads. "So good for making lists!" she said.

Katie opened three new cookbooks.

I slid open the envelope with my finger. Inside was a gift card.

The gift card was for Williams-Sonoma. And it was for fifty dollars!

I looked up and caught Alexis's eye, then Katie's, then Mia's. They all grinned. "But . . . ," I asked, confused. "How did she know . . . ?"

Alexis blushed. "Well, some secrets you do keep from friends. But just for a little while!" And we all laughed. I tucked the envelope into the purse Mom had let me borrow, and I smiled.

The wedding was going by so fast but so had the past few weeks. A lot of things had been burned, rushed, worried over, and hidden. All bad. I looked around at Mia's beautiful mom, all the pretty pink flowers, and saw how happy everyone was. Now everything was pretty good. I had my friends. I had people who loved me. I had brothers who weren't half bad most of the time.

"A toast!" I cried, lifting up my glass of lemonade.

Alexis, Katie, and Mia held up their glasses too.

"To friends!" I said.

"Here, here!" cried Mia.

"To no more secrets!" said Katie.

"To helping each other out always!" said Alexis.

"And," I said with a little bit of a giggle, "to the divine pink mixer that will soon be mine!"

Want another sweet cupcake?
Here's a sneak peek
of the fourth book in the

CUPCAKE 🧁 DIARIES

series:

Alexis
and the
perfect recipe

My Sister Takes the Cake

$\mathcal{M}$y name is Alexis Becker, and I'm the business mind (ha-ha) of the Cupcake Club. The club is a for-profit group that my best friends—Mia, Katie, and Emma—and I started, and we make money baking delicious cupcakes!

I love figuring out how to run a business and putting together the different building blocks—math, organization, and planning—that's why the girls can *count* on me for this kind of stuff. Plus, as you can tell, I love math-related puns! My friends are more creative with the cakes, so they come up with the designs and other artistic stuff. My one specialty, though, is fondant. I am very good at making little flowers and designs out of that firm frosting. Otherwise, I'm mostly crunching numbers and wondering how to make money. Mmm . . . money!

If the Cupcake Club was an equation, it would look like this:

$$(Four\ girls + supplies)\ x\ clients = \$\$\$\$$$

Or really, more like this:

$$(Profit - supplies)\ /\ 4 = \$$$

We actually have lots of fun doing it. Most of our clients are really nice people, which is much more than I can say for our last client: my sister, Dylan. I can practically still hear her fuming.

"It is *my* party, *I* am the one turning sixteen, and I have budgeted *everything* down to the last party favor. I know *exactly* what I'm doing!" She was talking to our mom behind closed doors, but I heard every word since I was right outside her bedroom!

Dylan never gets out-of-control mad; she's always in total control. Except that ever since she'd started planning her sweet sixteen party (which was now four and a half weeks away), she'd been cranky *a lot*. But she never raises her voice when she gets mad. She lowers it to a whisper, and you can hear the chill in it, as if actual icicles were hanging from the words. I had to put my ear to her bedroom door to hear everything that was being said. Knowledge is power; that's one of my mottoes, and I need all the information I can get. About everything.

My mother was sounding kind of amused by the fight, which was about two things: the guest list for the party and the cake. I had an interest in the outcome of both, since I wanted to be able to invite my best friends, and *we* wanted to bake the dessert for the party. (It wasn't about the money as we wouldn't charge a lot; it's just that it would be great exposure for our business!)

I could picture Mom trying to not smile and to take Dylan seriously. "Darling, I know how careful you are, and I am impressed, as always, by your work," she said. "I admire your attention to detail on these spreadsheets. However, not everything will be according to *your* plan, as your father and I also have a say in what works best for this family. Now let's take a look at this guest list again."

I grinned. Mom was on *my* side.

DID YOU
LOVE THIS BOOK?